THIS BOOK BELONGS TO

THANKS TO PHILIPPA, MY FAMILY,
MARTHA, JULES AND EVERYBODY AT NOBROW

THIS PAPERBACK EDITION PUBLISHED IN 2019.
FIRST PUBLISHED IN 2015 BY FLYING EYE BOOKS, AN IMPRINT OF NOBROW LTD.
27 WESTGATE STREET, LONDON, E8 3RL

ORIGINALLY APPEARING IN PRINT IN 2010 AS HILDAFOLK © 2010 NOBROW LTD AND LUKE PEARSON.

10 8 6 4 2 3 5 7 9

PUBLISHED IN THE US BY NOBROW INC, IN 2018.
PRINTED IN POLAND ON FSC® CERTIFIED PAPER

ISBN: 978-1-912497-54-6
WWW.FLYINGEYEBOOKS.COM

HILDA'S DRAWINGS APPEARING ON P.32-35 BY MARTHA NORMAN

LUKE PEARSON

HILDA
AND
THE TROLL

FLYING EYE BOOKS
LONDON – NEW YORK

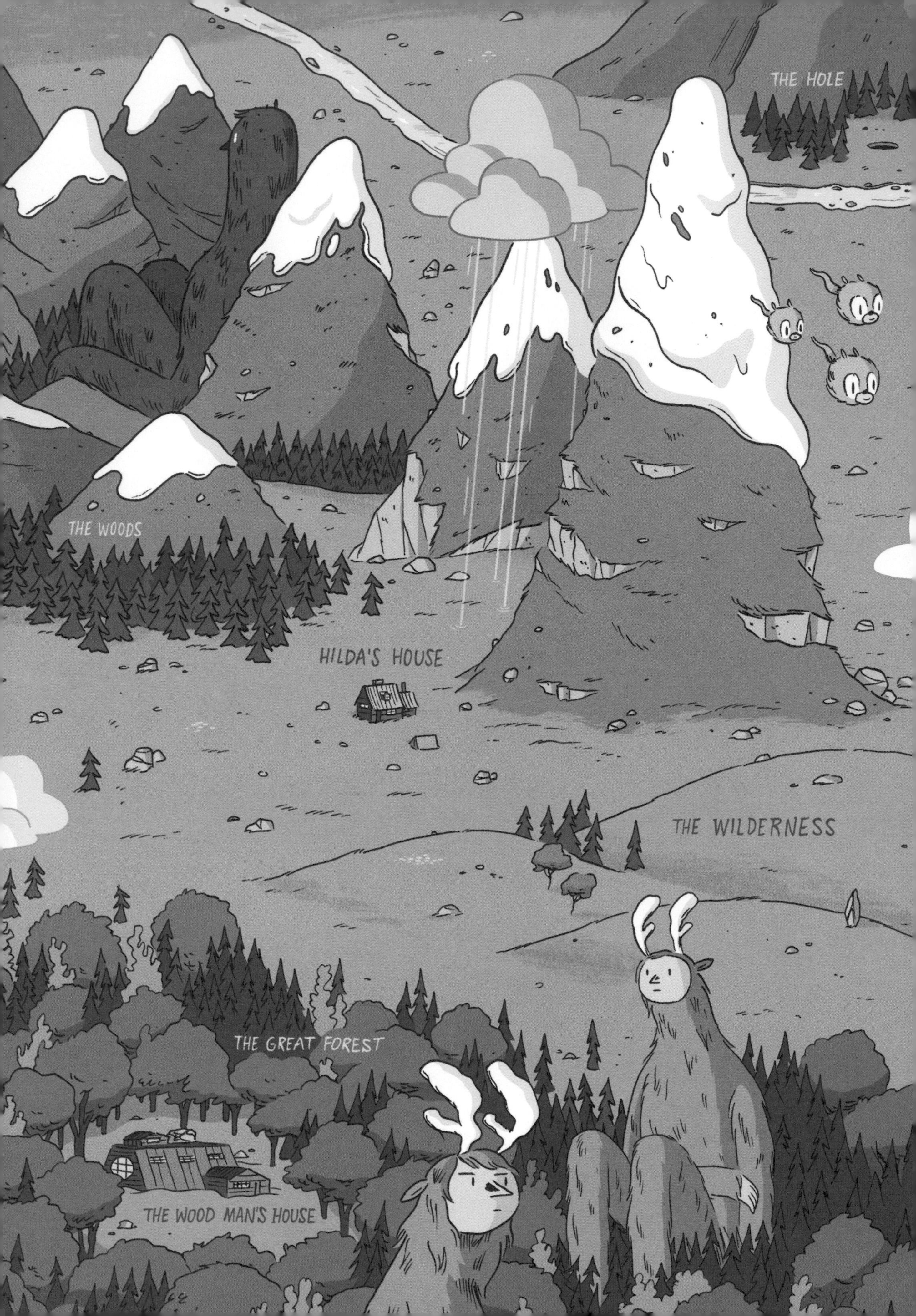
THE HOLE
THE WOODS
HILDA'S HOUSE
THE WILDERNESS
THE GREAT FOREST
THE WOOD MAN'S HOUSE

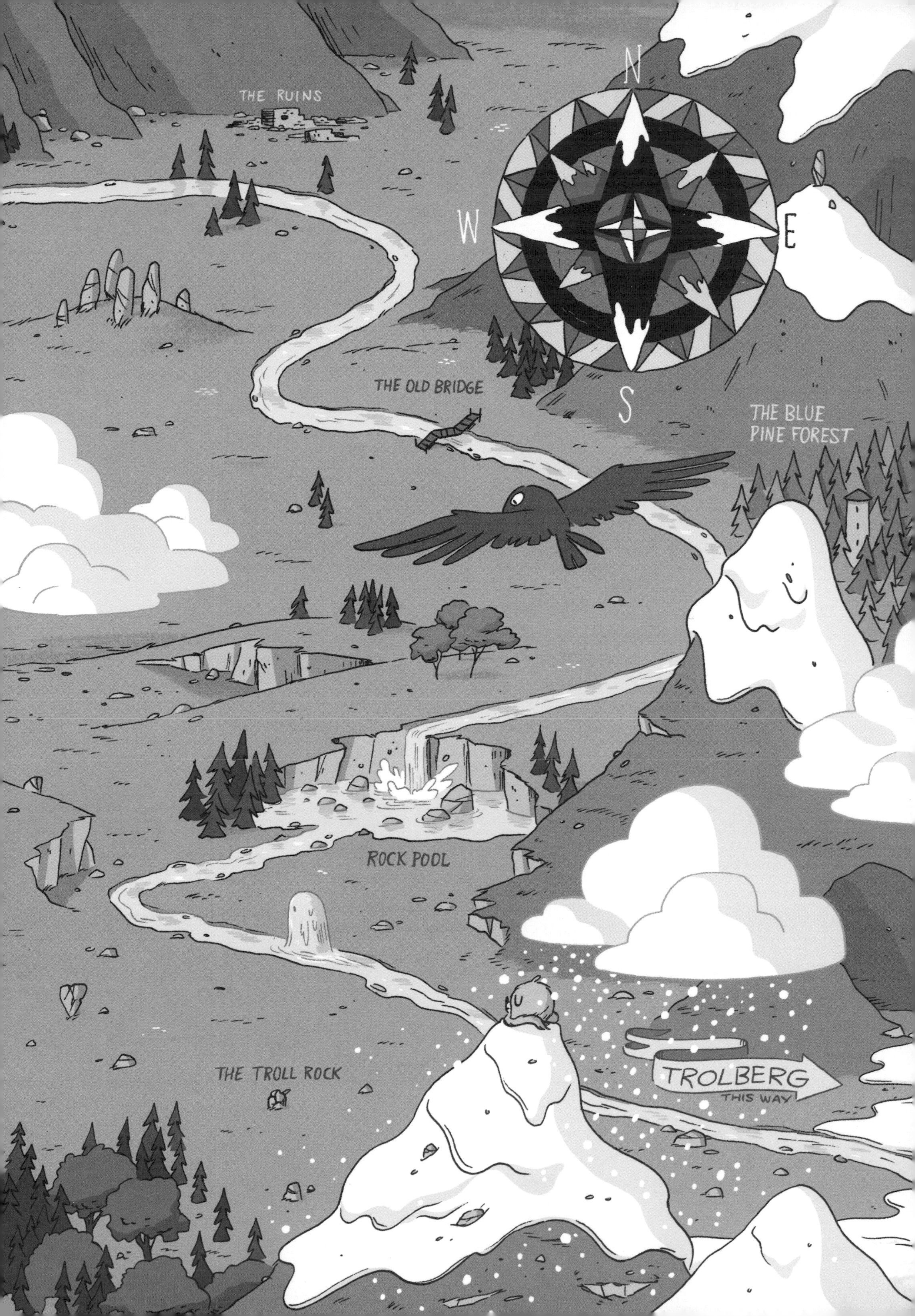
N
W
E
S
THE RUINS
THE OLD BRIDGE
THE BLUE
PINE FOREST
ROCK POOL
THE TROLL ROCK
TROLBERG
THIS WAY

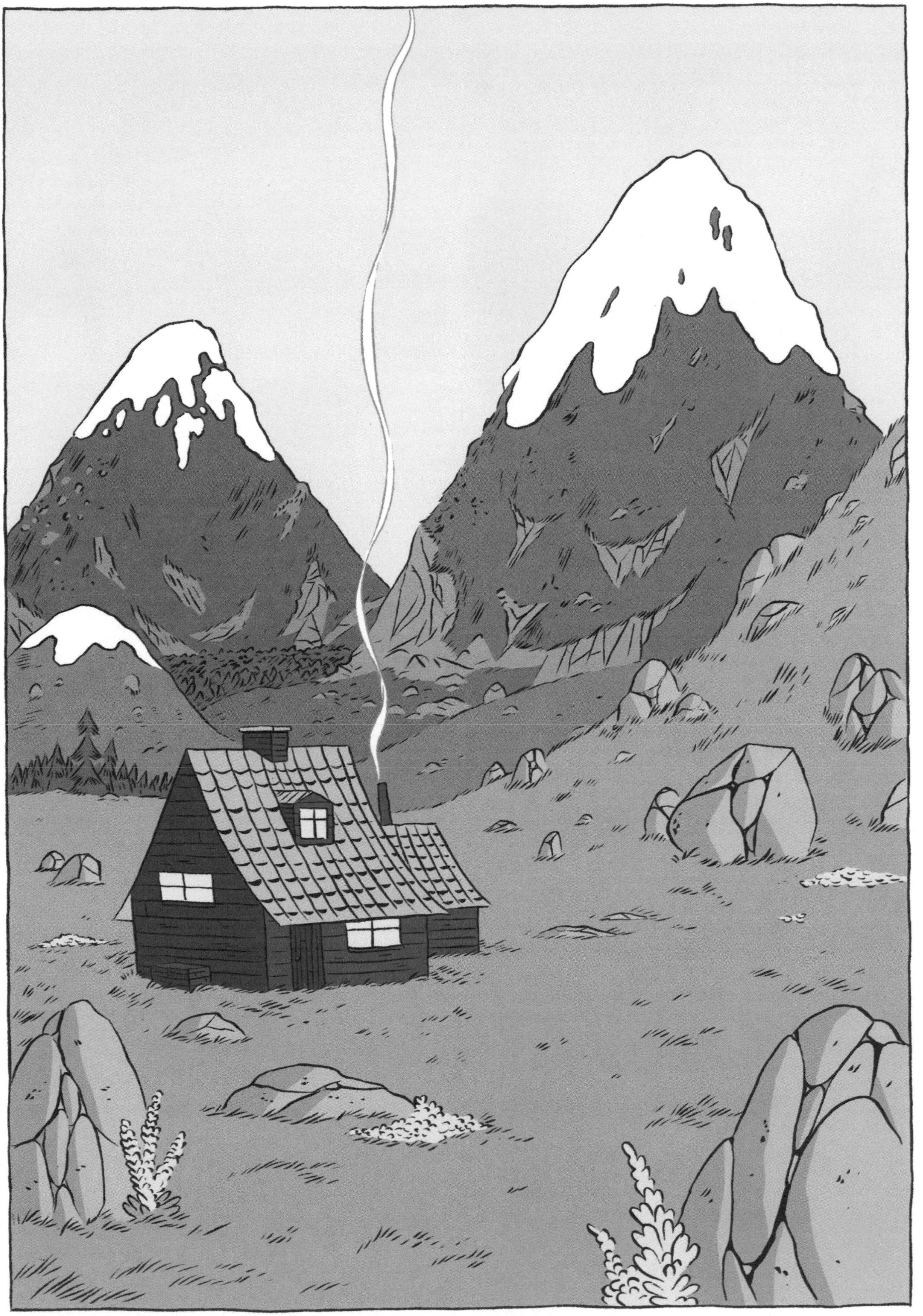

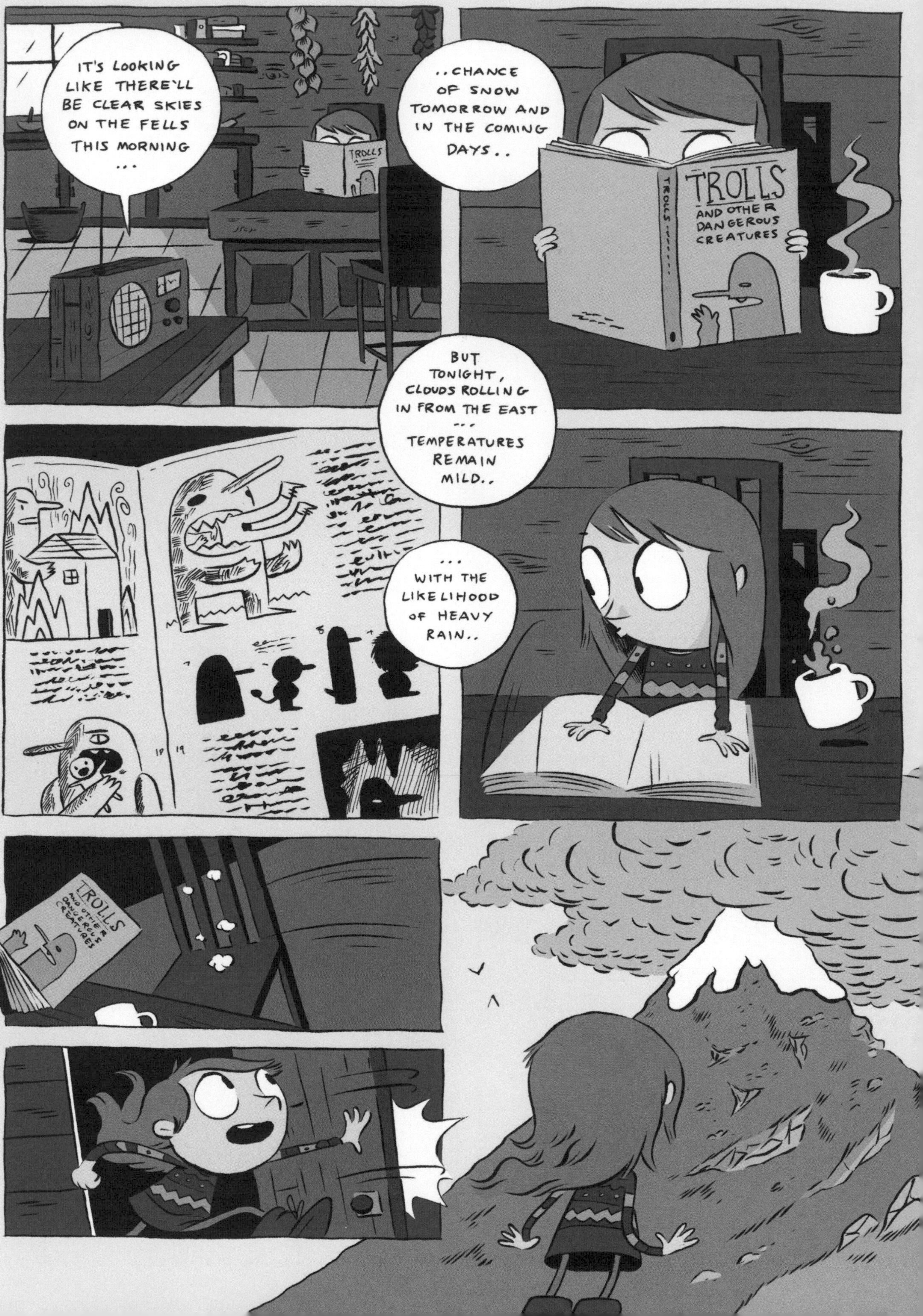
IT'S LOOKING LIKE THERE'LL BE CLEAR SKIES ON THE FELLS THIS MORNING ...
TROLLS
..CHANCE OF SNOW TOMORROW AND IN THE COMING DAYS..
TROLLS AND OTHER DANGEROUS CREATURES
BUT TONIGHT, CLOUDS ROLLING IN FROM THE EAST ... TEMPERATURES REMAIN MILD..
... WITH THE LIKELIHOOD OF HEAVY RAIN..
TROLLS AND OTHER DANGEROUS CREATURES

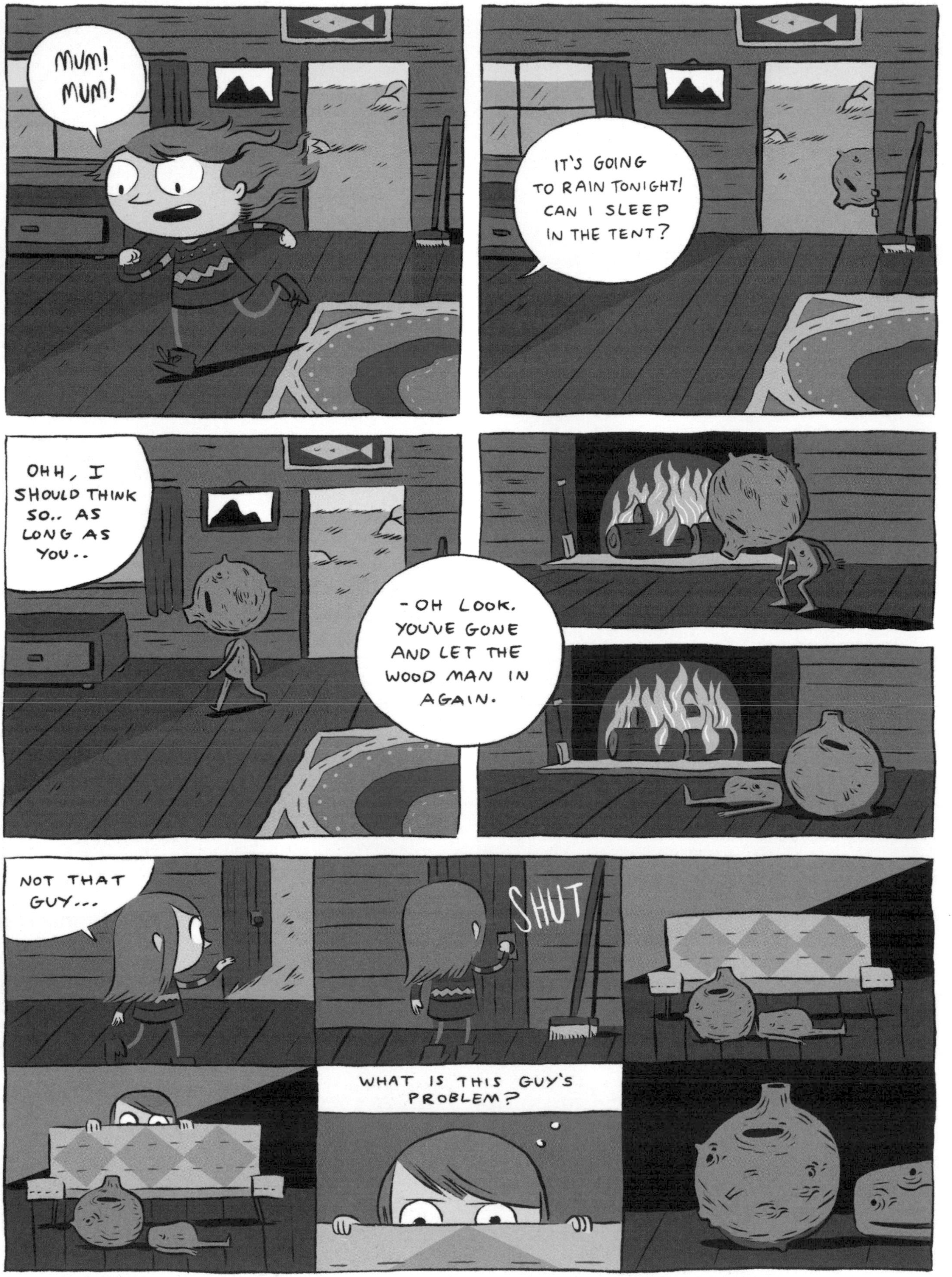
MUM! MUM!
IT'S GOING TO RAIN TONIGHT! CAN I SLEEP IN THE TENT?
OHH, I SHOULD THINK SO.. AS LONG AS YOU..
-OH LOOK. YOU'VE GONE AND LET THE WOOD MAN IN AGAIN.
NOT THAT GUY...
SHUT
WHAT IS THIS GUY'S PROBLEM?

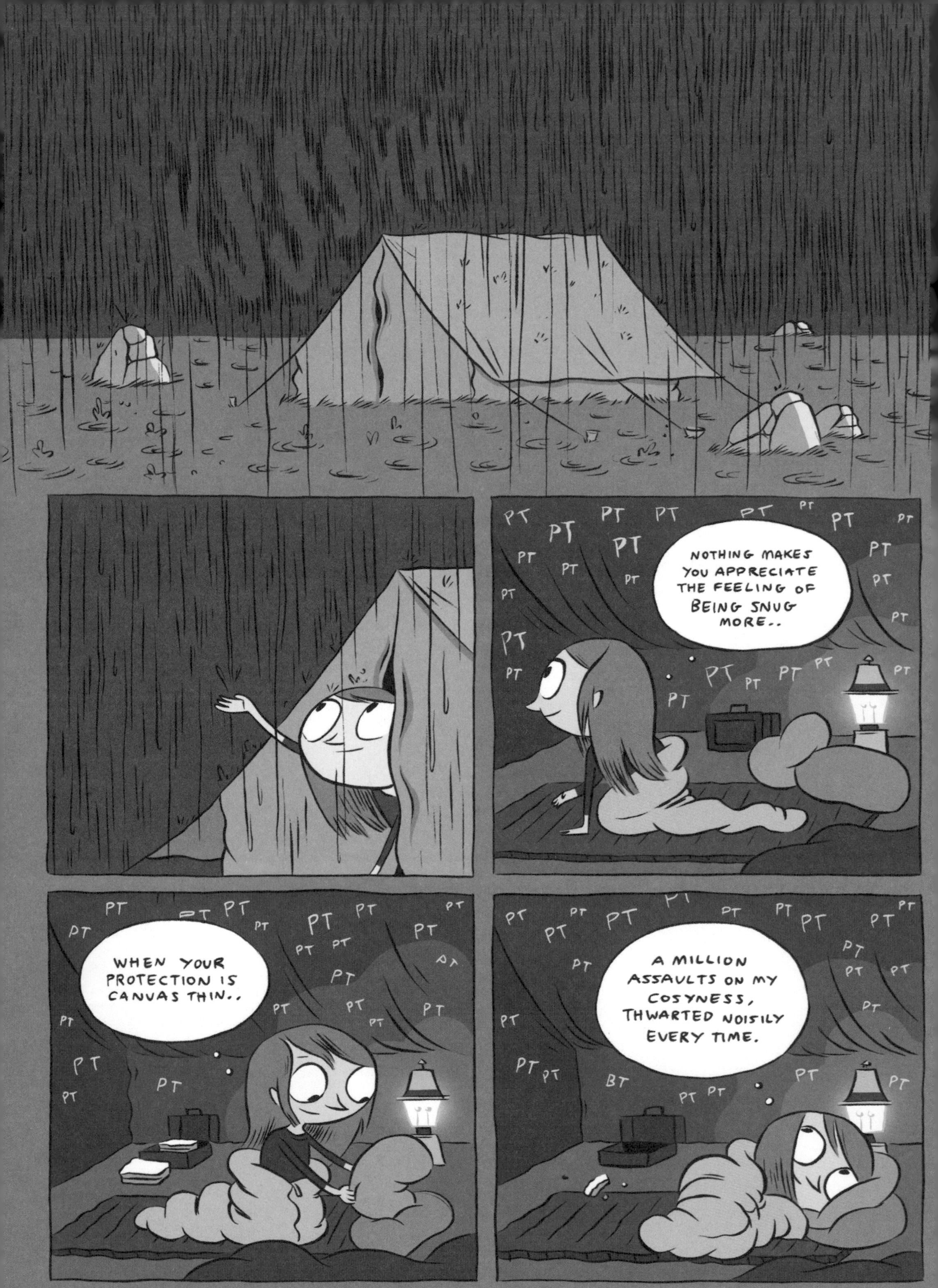
NOTHING MAKES YOU APPRECIATE THE FEELING OF BEING SNUG MORE..
WHEN YOUR PROTECTION IS CANVAS THIN..
A MILLION ASSAULTS ON MY COSYNESS, THWARTED NOISILY EVERY TIME.

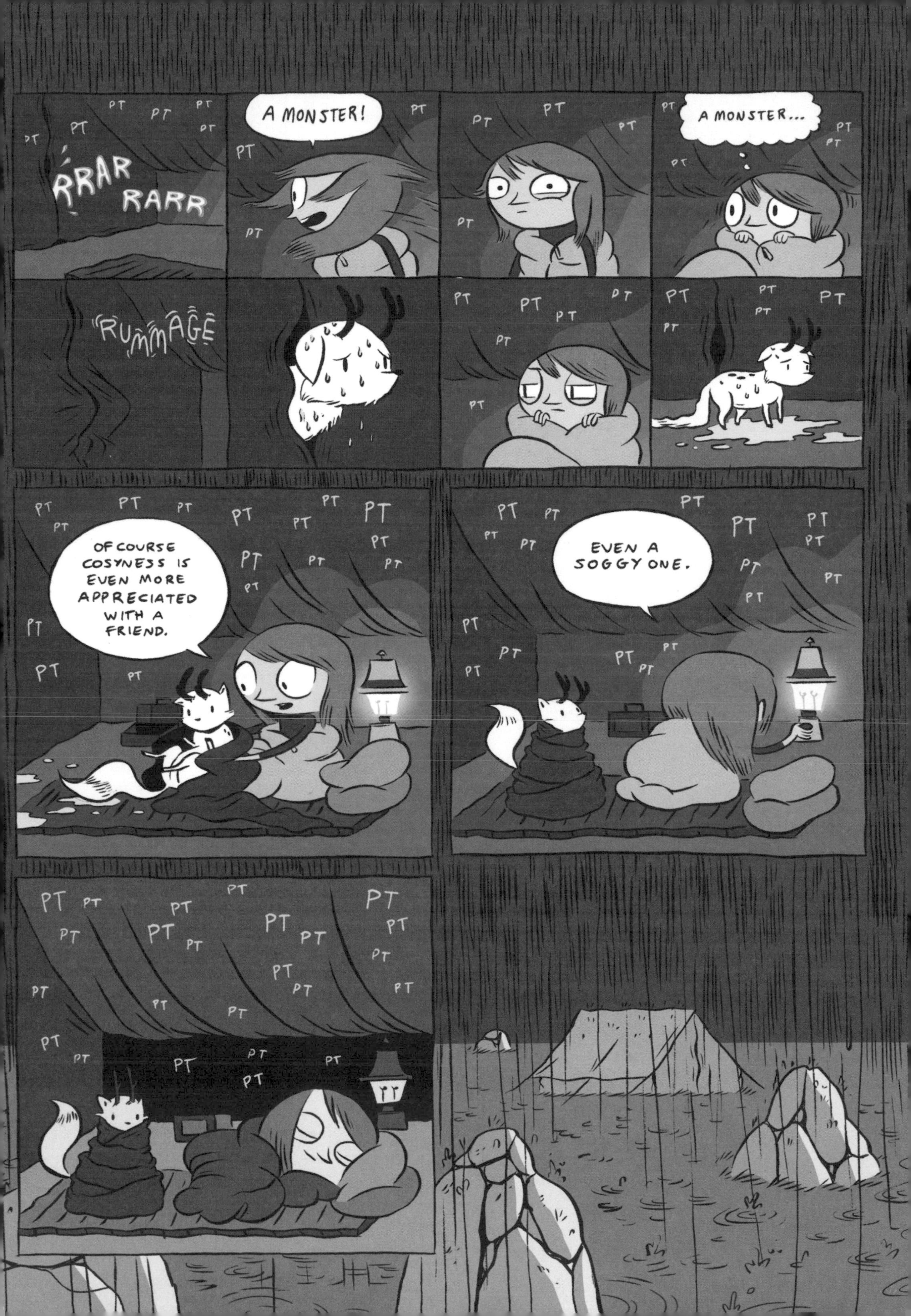

PT PT PT PT PT PT
RRAR RARR
A MONSTER!
A MONSTER...
RUMMAGE
OF COURSE COSYNESS IS EVEN MORE APPRECIATED WITH A FRIEND.
EVEN A SOGGY ONE.

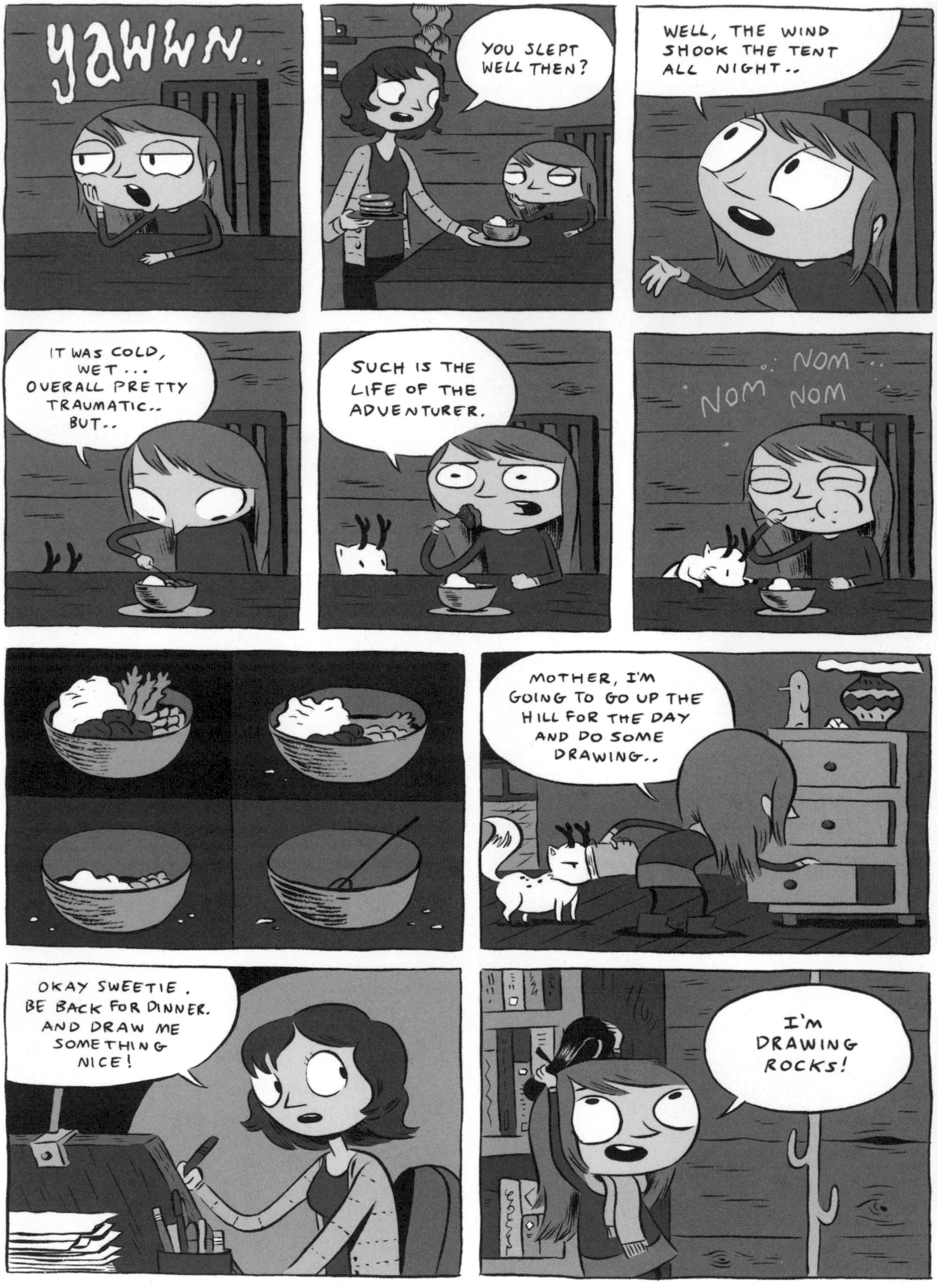
YAWWN..
YOU SLEPT WELL THEN?
WELL, THE WIND SHOOK THE TENT ALL NIGHT..
IT WAS COLD, WET... OVERALL PRETTY TRAUMATIC.. BUT..
SUCH IS THE LIFE OF THE ADVENTURER.
NOM NOM NOM
MOTHER, I'M GOING TO GO UP THE HILL FOR THE DAY AND DO SOME DRAWING..
OKAY SWEETIE. BE BACK FOR DINNER. AND DRAW ME SOMETHING NICE!
I'M DRAWING ROCKS!

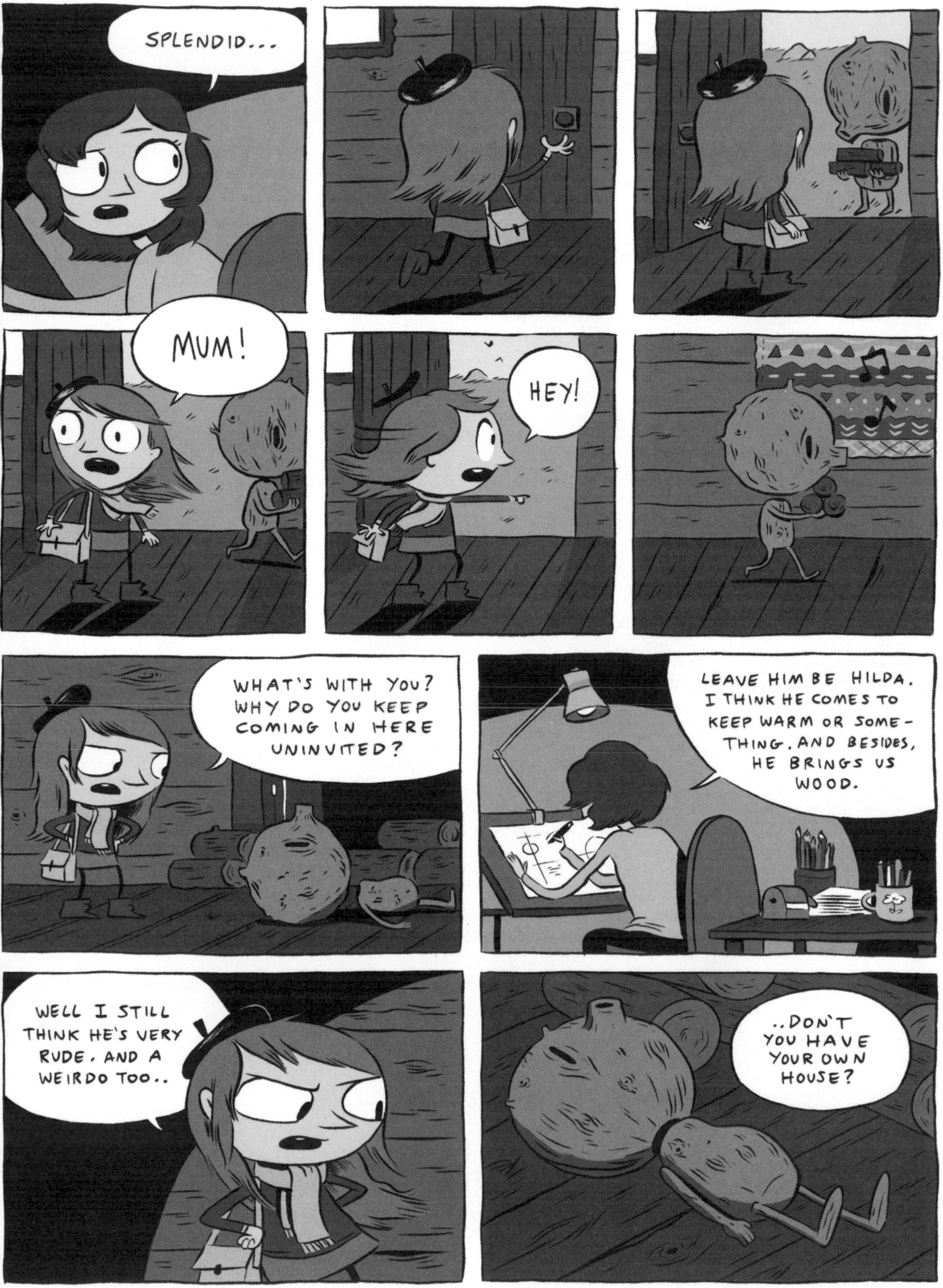
SPLENDID...
MUM!
HEY!
WHAT'S WITH YOU? WHY DO YOU KEEP COMING IN HERE UNINVITED?
LEAVE HIM BE HILDA. I THINK HE COMES TO KEEP WARM OR SOME-THING. AND BESIDES, HE BRINGS US WOOD.
WELL I STILL THINK HE'S VERY RUDE. AND A WEIRDO TOO..
..DON'T YOU HAVE YOUR OWN HOUSE?

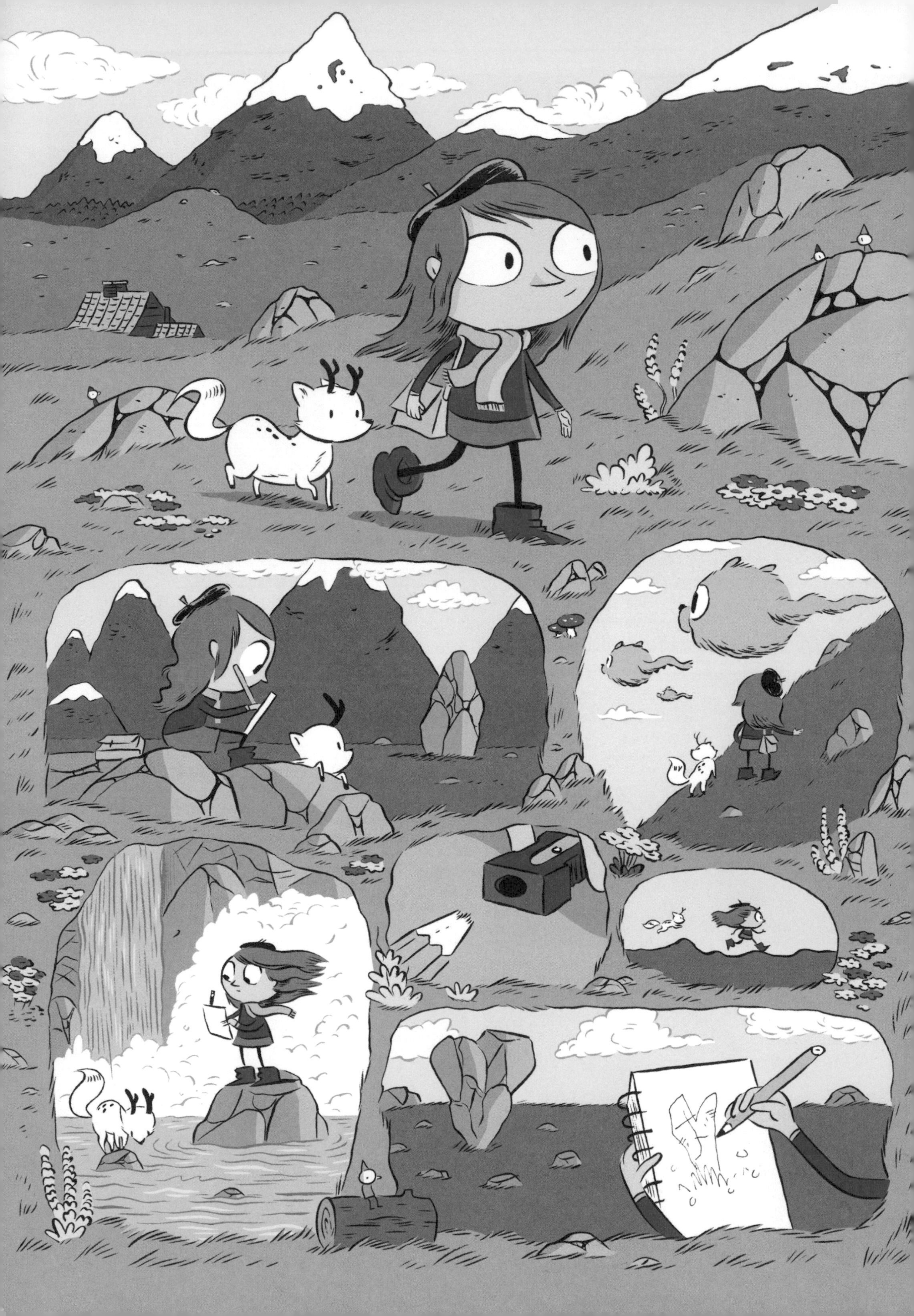

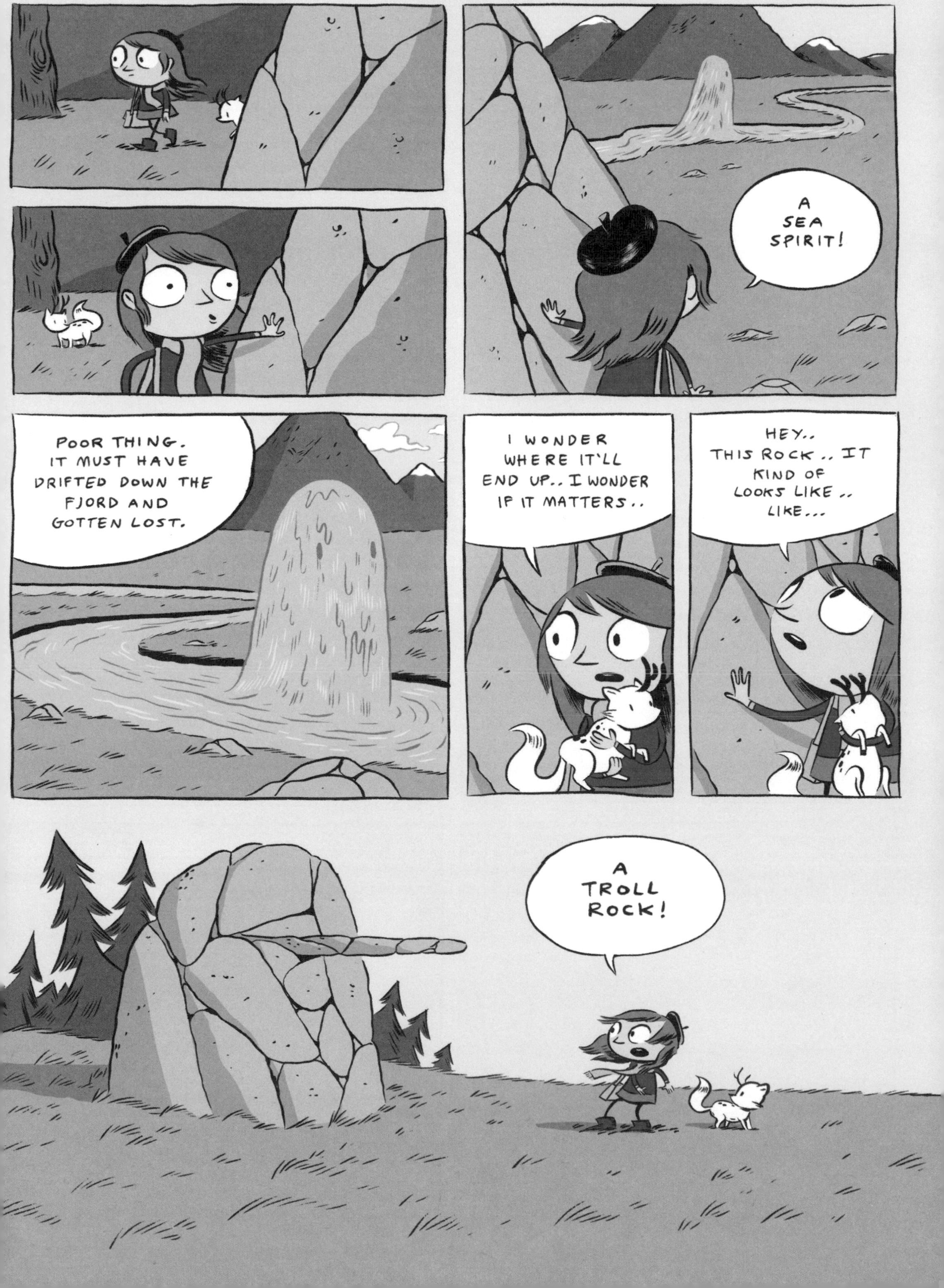
A SEA SPIRIT!
POOR THING. IT MUST HAVE DRIFTED DOWN THE FJORD AND GOTTEN LOST.
I WONDER WHERE IT'LL END UP.. I WONDER IF IT MATTERS..
HEY.. THIS ROCK .. IT KIND OF LOOKS LIKE .. LIKE...
A TROLL ROCK!

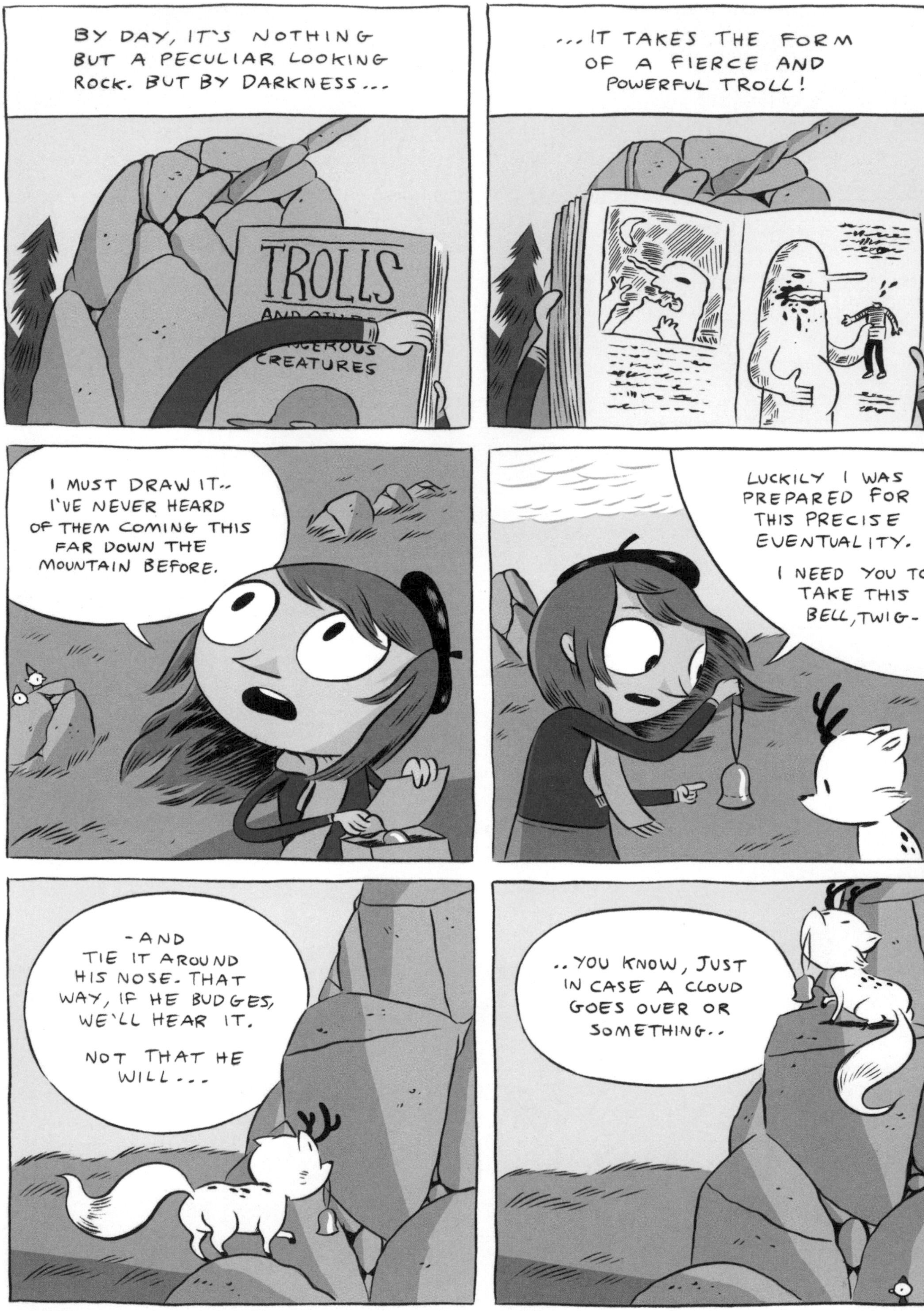
BY DAY, IT'S NOTHING BUT A PECULIAR LOOKING ROCK. BUT BY DARKNESS...
TROLLS
CREATURES
...IT TAKES THE FORM OF A FIERCE AND POWERFUL TROLL!
I MUST DRAW IT.. I'VE NEVER HEARD OF THEM COMING THIS FAR DOWN THE MOUNTAIN BEFORE.
LUCKILY I WAS PREPARED FOR THIS PRECISE EVENTUALITY.
I NEED YOU TO TAKE THIS BELL, TWIG-
-AND TIE IT AROUND HIS NOSE. THAT WAY, IF HE BUDGES, WE'LL HEAR IT.
NOT THAT HE WILL...
..YOU KNOW, JUST IN CASE A CLOUD GOES OVER OR SOMETHING..

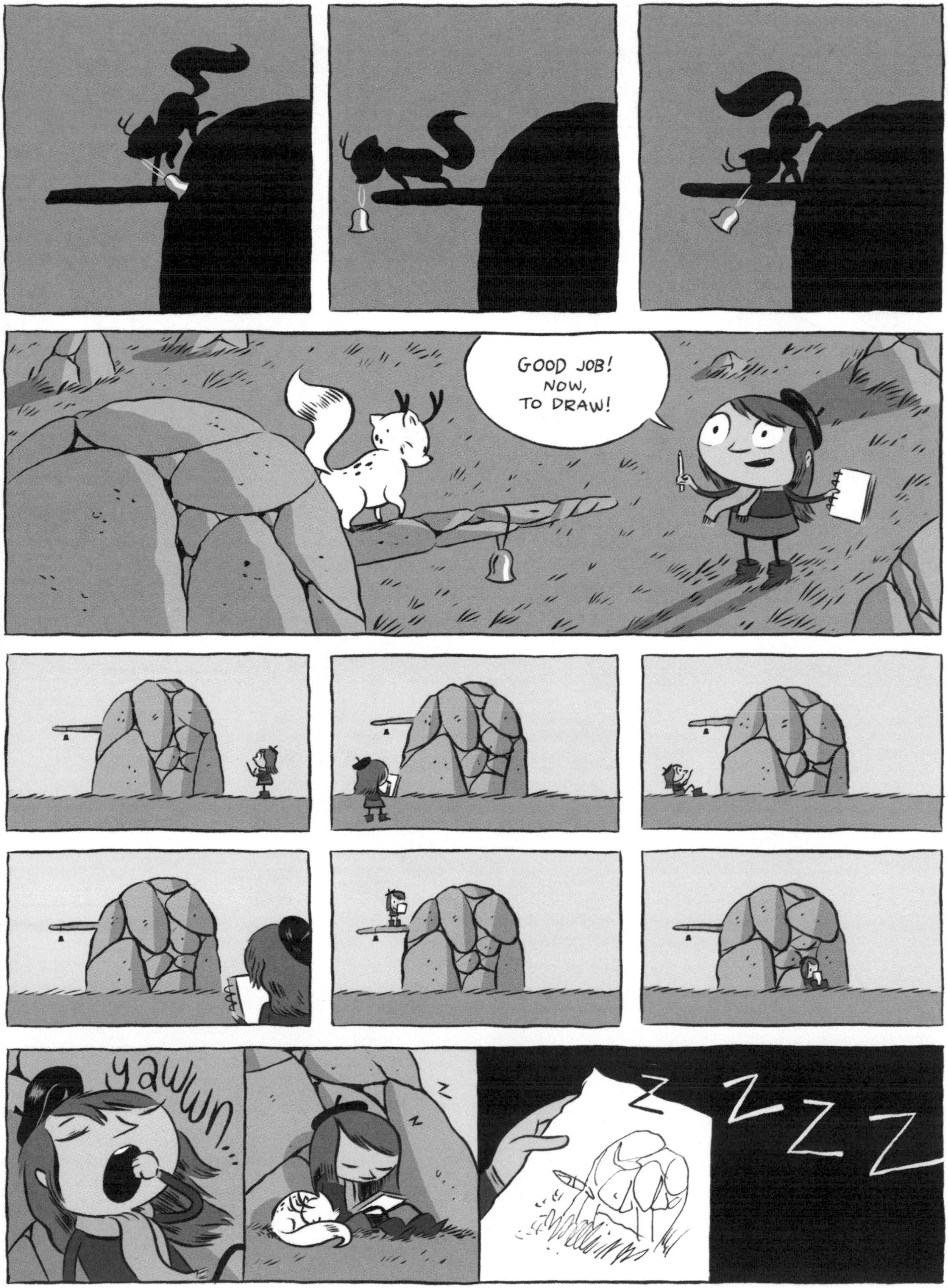
GOOD JOB! NOW, TO DRAW!
yawwn
Z
Z
Z Z Z Z

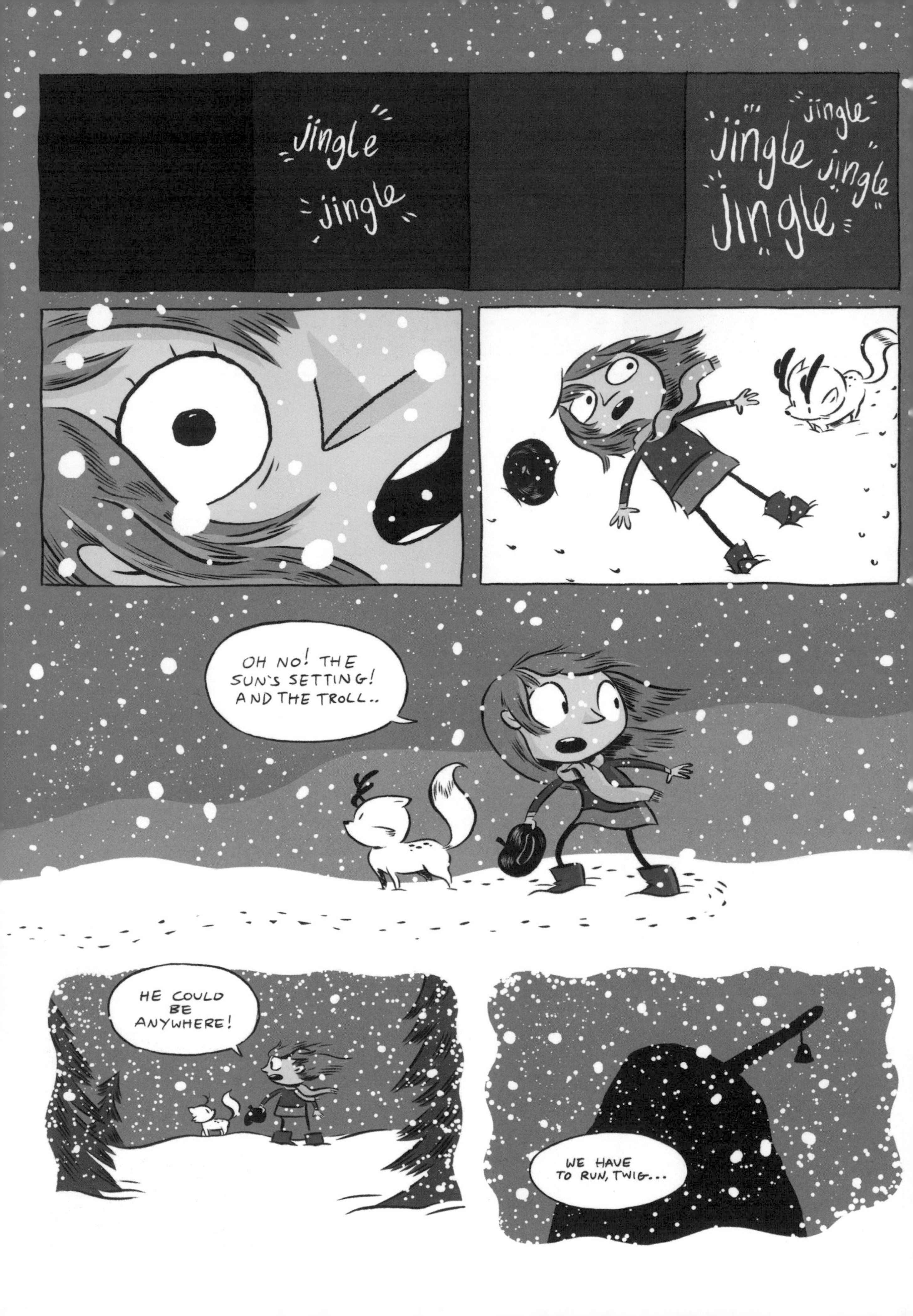

jingle
jingle
jingle
jingle
jingle
jingle
OH NO! THE SUN'S SETTING! AND THE TROLL..
HE COULD BE ANYWHERE!
WE HAVE TO RUN, TWIG...

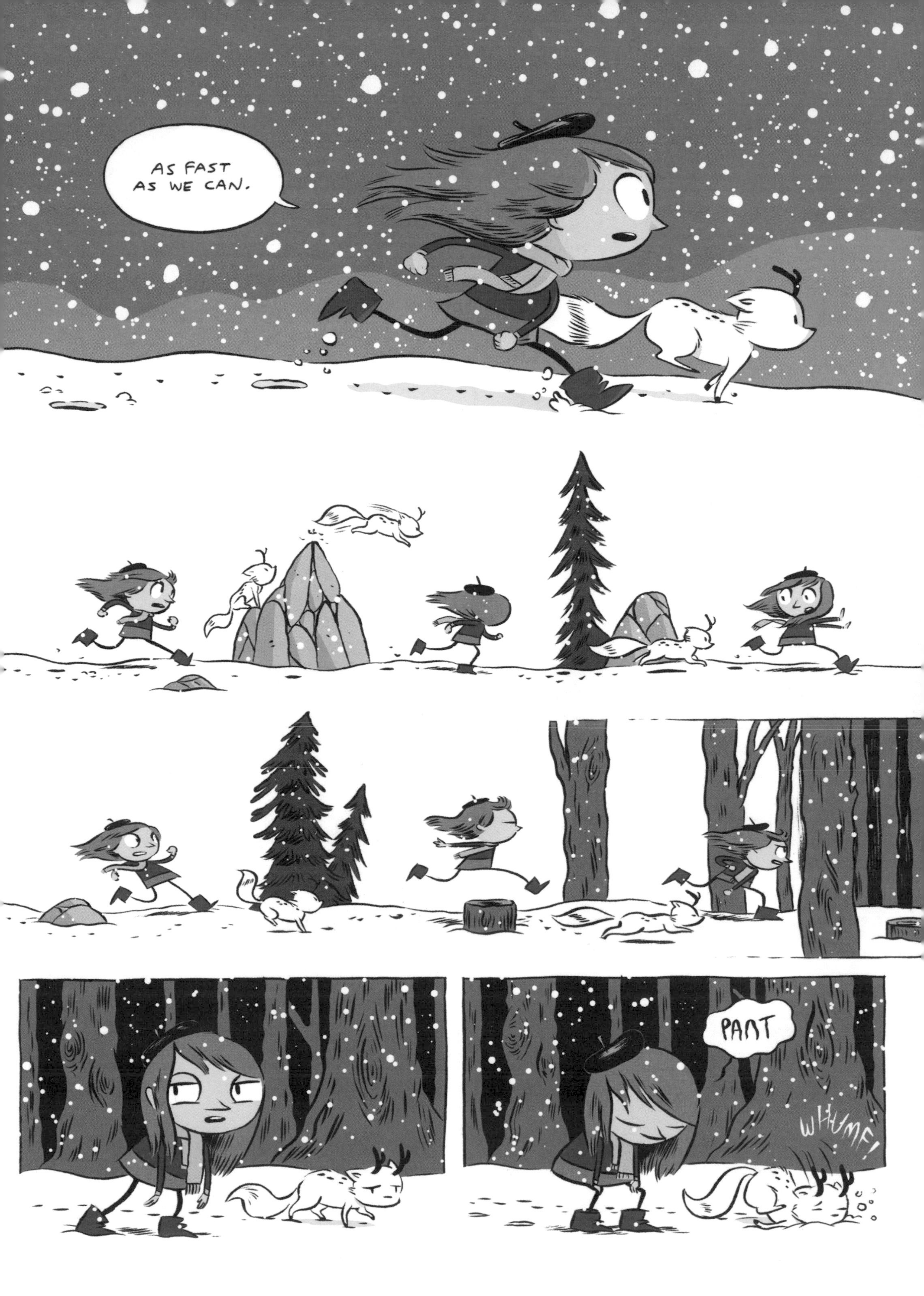
AS FAST AS WE CAN.
PANT
WHUMF!

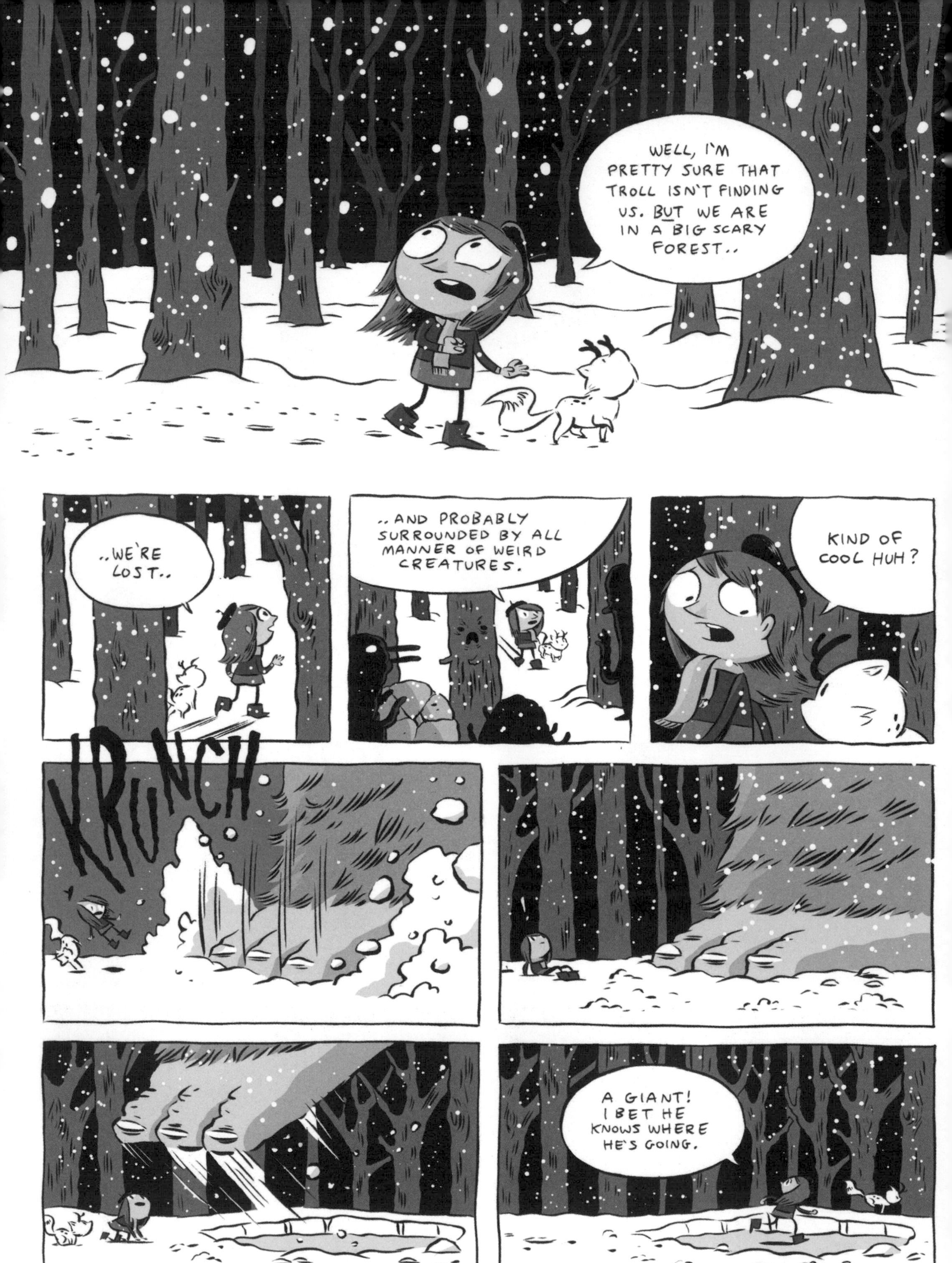
WELL, I'M PRETTY SURE THAT TROLL ISN'T FINDING US. BUT WE ARE IN A BIG SCARY FOREST..
..WE'RE LOST..
..AND PROBABLY SURROUNDED BY ALL MANNER OF WEIRD CREATURES.
KIND OF COOL HUH?
KRUNCH
A GIANT! I BET HE KNOWS WHERE HE'S GOING.

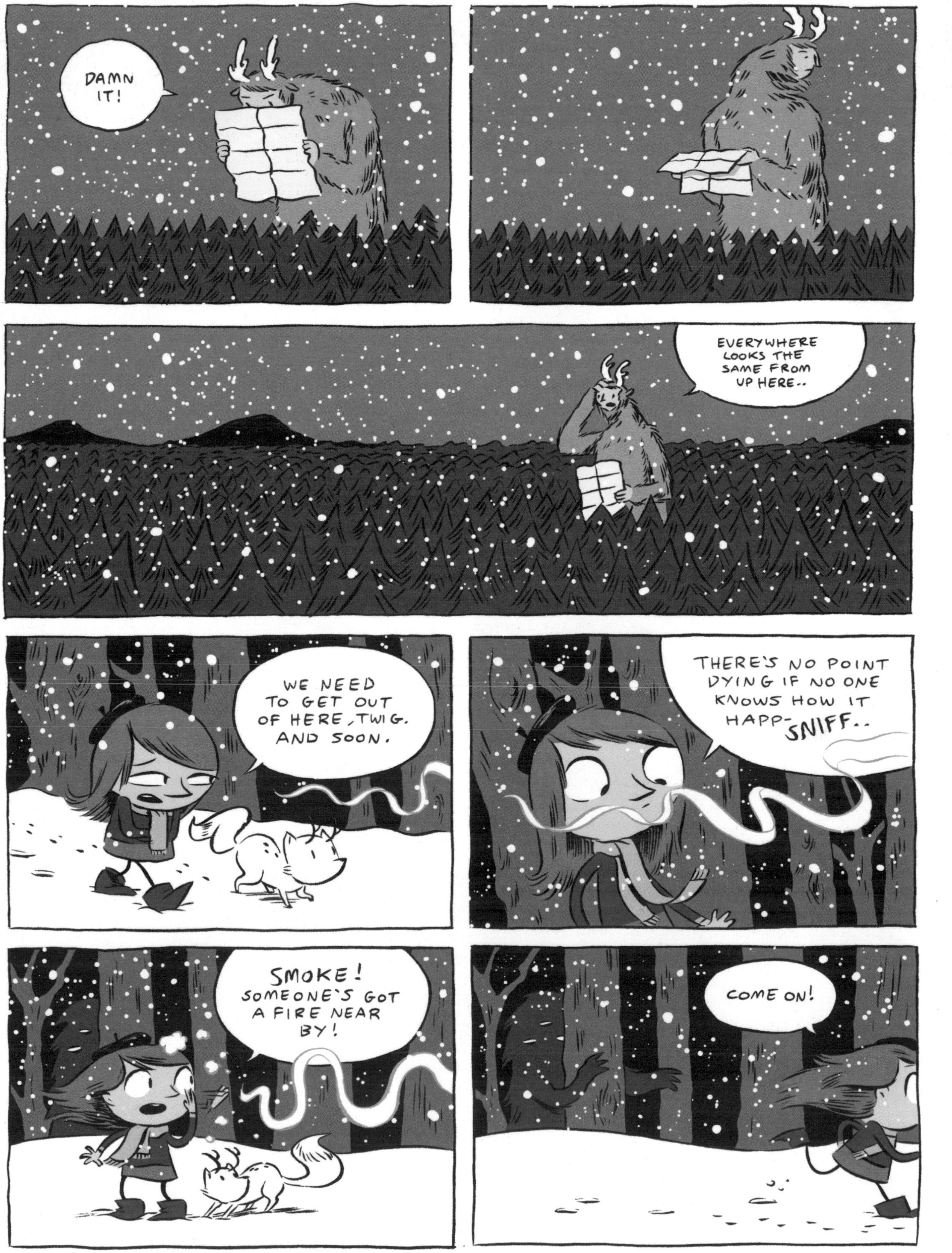
DAMN IT!
EVERYWHERE LOOKS THE SAME FROM UP HERE..
WE NEED TO GET OUT OF HERE, TWIG. AND SOON.
THERE'S NO POINT DYING IF NO ONE KNOWS HOW IT HAPP-SNIFF..
SMOKE! SOMEONE'S GOT A FIRE NEAR BY!
COME ON!

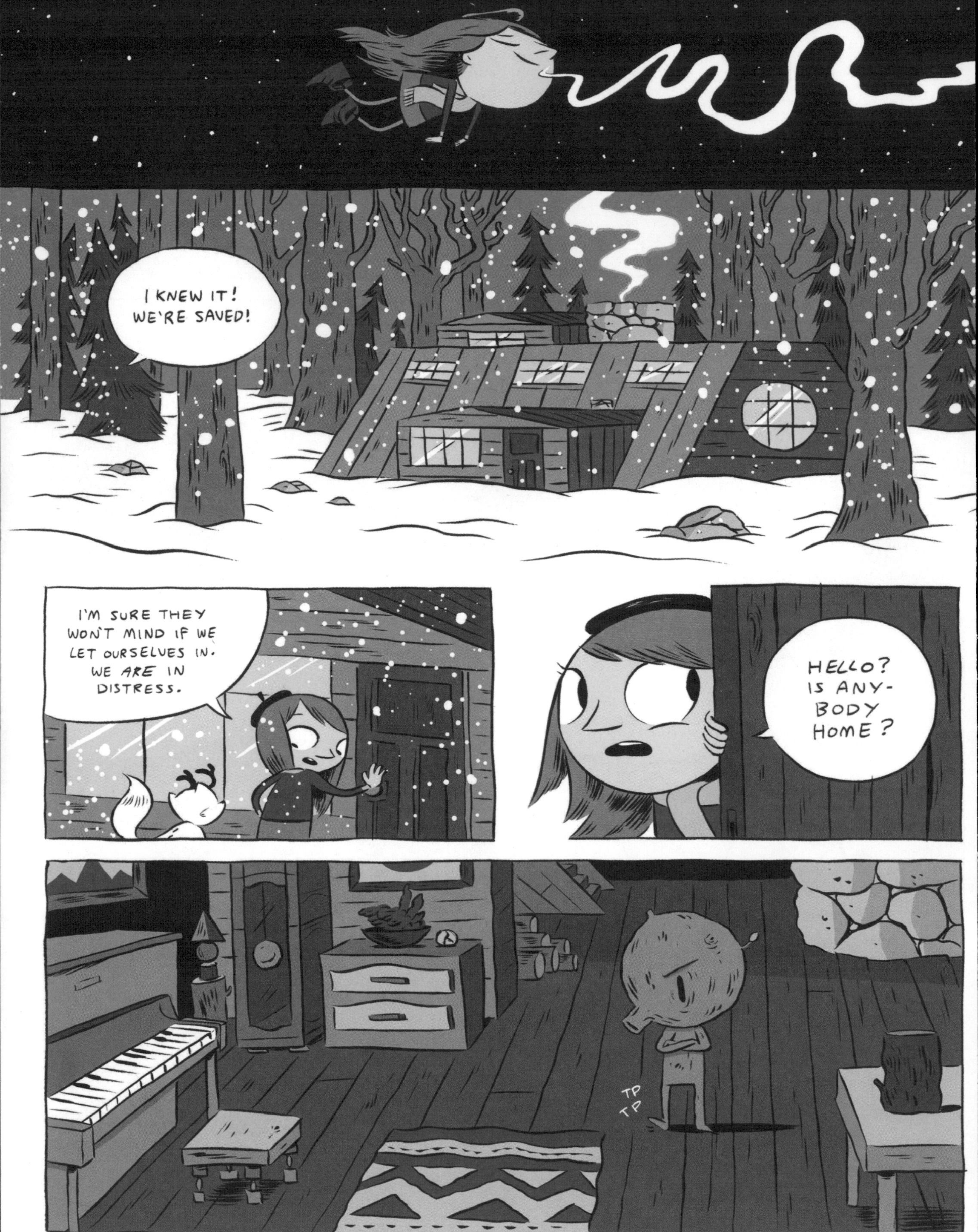
I KNEW IT! WE'RE SAVED!
I'M SURE THEY WON'T MIND IF WE LET OURSELVES IN. WE ARE IN DISTRESS.
HELLO? IS ANY-BODY HOME?
TP TP

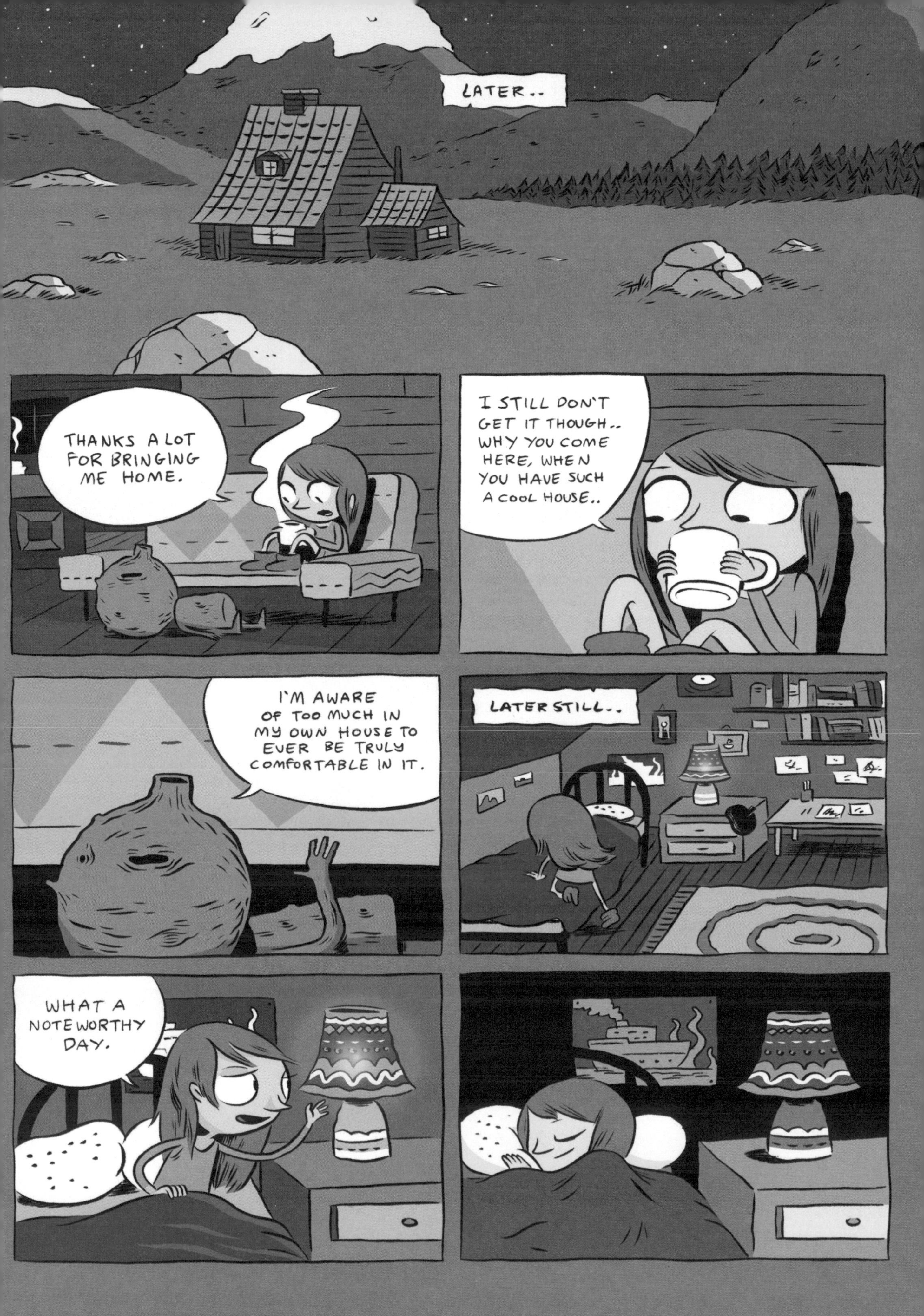
LATER..
THANKS A LOT FOR BRINGING ME HOME.
I STILL DON'T GET IT THOUGH.. WHY YOU COME HERE, WHEN YOU HAVE SUCH A COOL HOUSE..
I'M AWARE OF TOO MUCH IN MY OWN HOUSE TO EVER BE TRULY COMFORTABLE IN IT.
LATER STILL..
WHAT A NOTEWORTHY DAY.

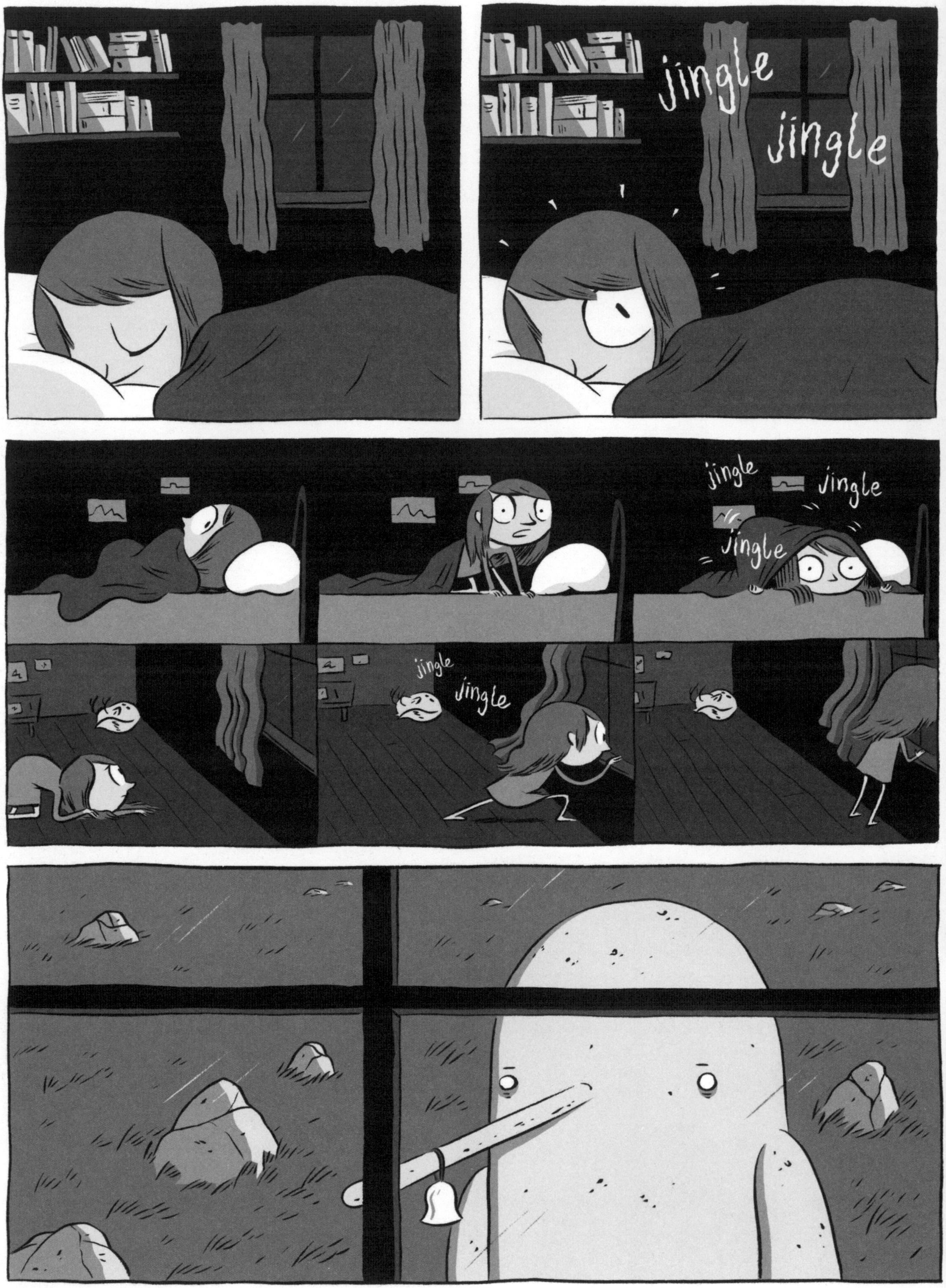
jingle
jingle
jingle
jingle
jingle
jingle
jingle

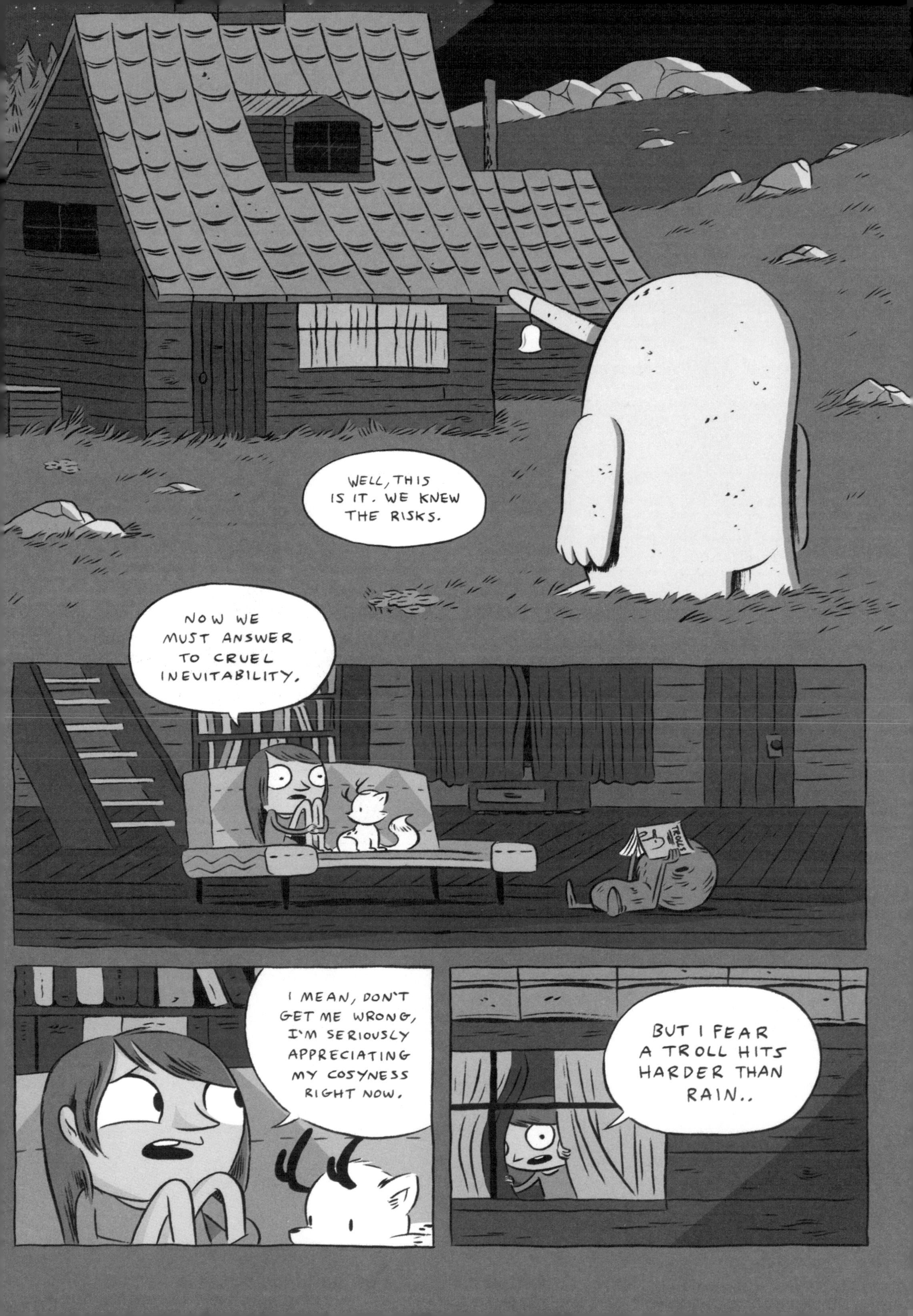
WELL, THIS IS IT. WE KNEW THE RISKS.
NOW WE MUST ANSWER TO CRUEL INEVITABILITY.
I MEAN, DON'T GET ME WRONG, I'M SERIOUSLY APPRECIATING MY COSYNESS RIGHT NOW.
BUT I FEAR A TROLL HITS HARDER THAN RAIN..

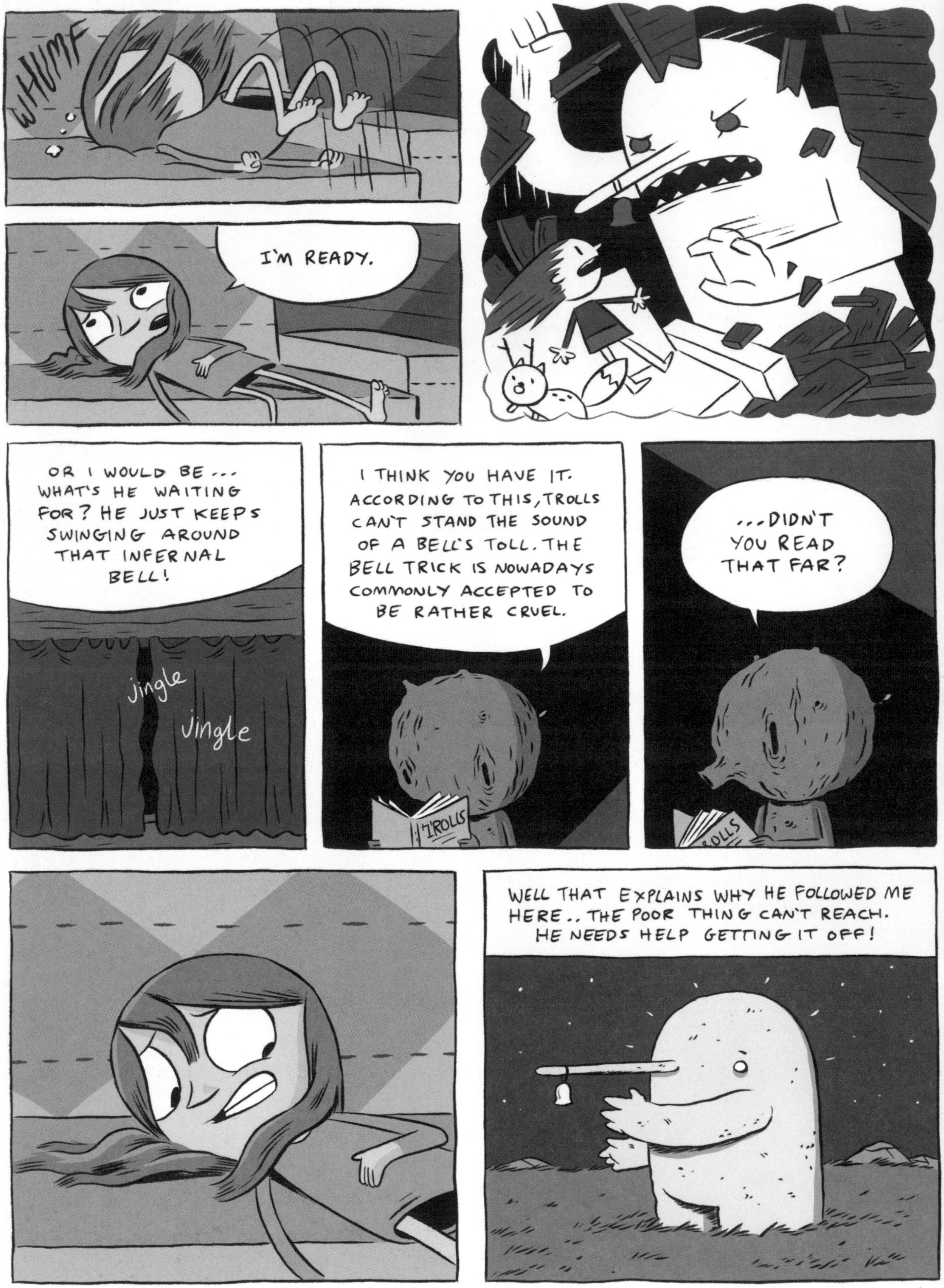
WHUMF
I'M READY.
OR I WOULD BE... WHAT'S HE WAITING FOR? HE JUST KEEPS SWINGING AROUND THAT INFERNAL BELL!
jingle
jingle
I THINK YOU HAVE IT. ACCORDING TO THIS, TROLLS CAN'T STAND THE SOUND OF A BELL'S TOLL. THE BELL TRICK IS NOWADAYS COMMONLY ACCEPTED TO BE RATHER CRUEL.
TROLLS
...DIDN'T YOU READ THAT FAR?
WELL THAT EXPLAINS WHY HE FOLLOWED ME HERE.. THE POOR THING CAN'T REACH. HE NEEDS HELP GETTING IT OFF!

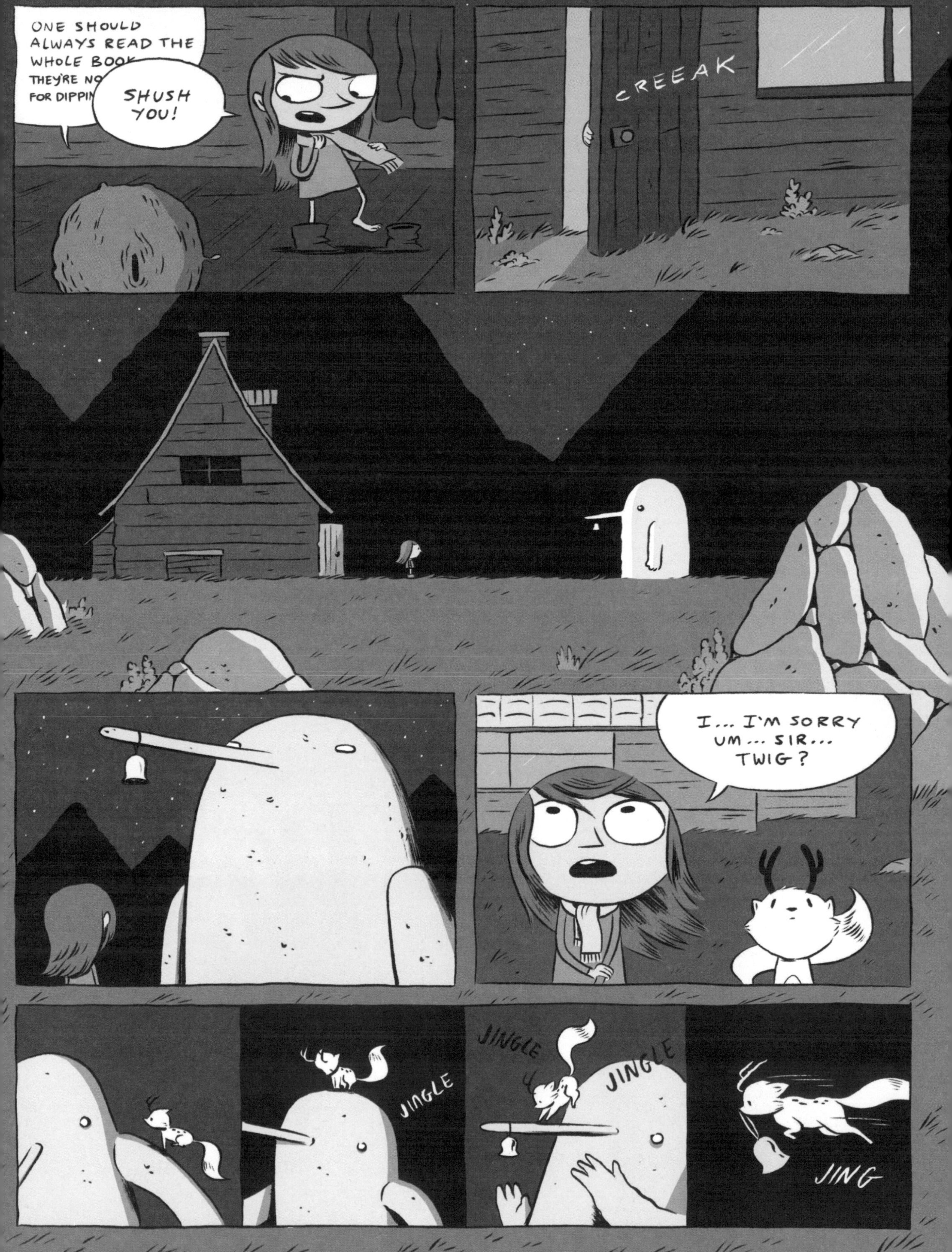

ONE SHOULD ALWAYS READ THE WHOLE BOOK
SHUSH YOU!
CREEAK
I... I'M SORRY UM... SIR... TWIG?
JINGLE
JINGLE
JINGLE
JING

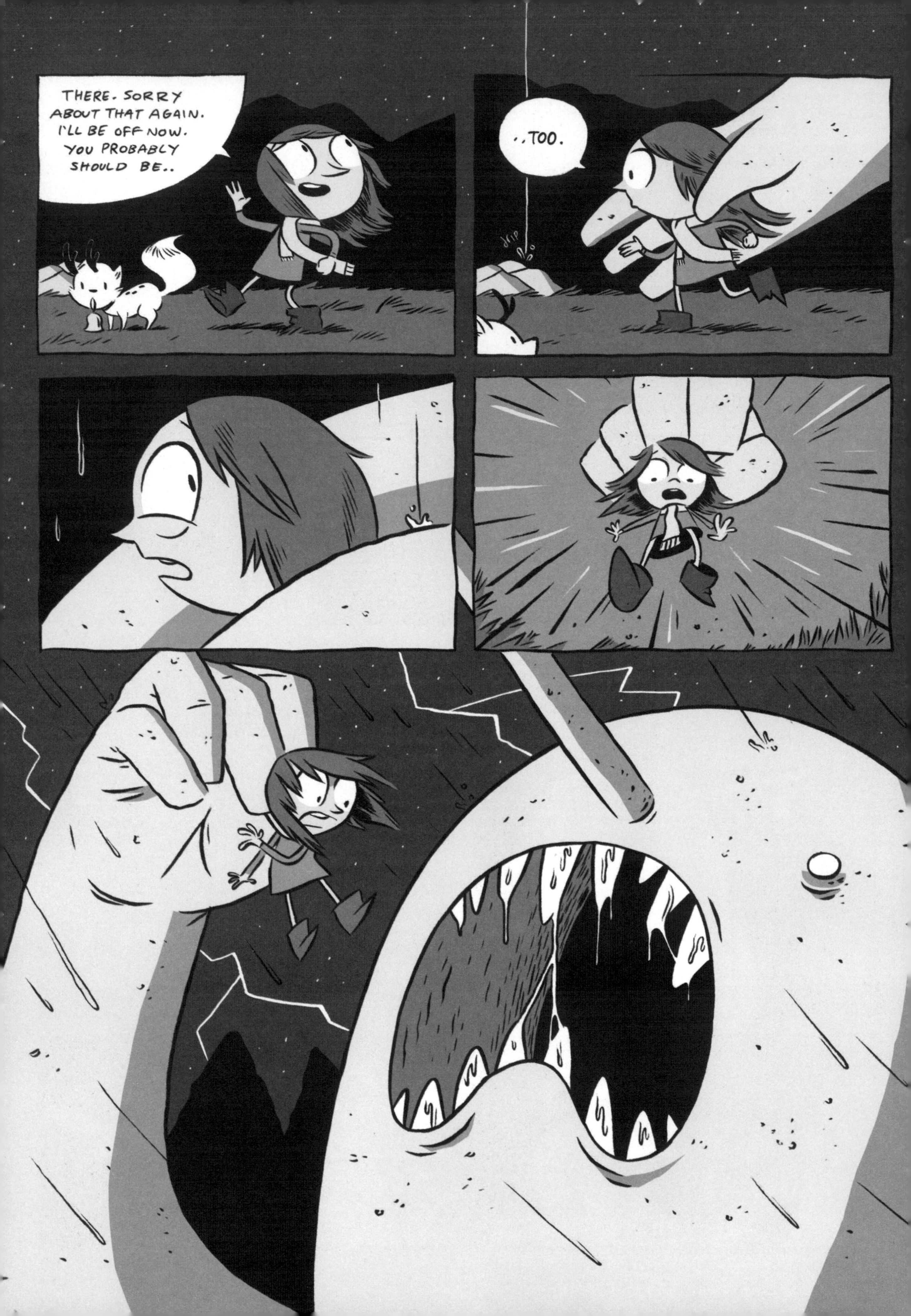
THERE. SORRY ABOUT THAT AGAIN. I'LL BE OFF NOW. YOU PROBABLY SHOULD BE..
..TOO.
drip

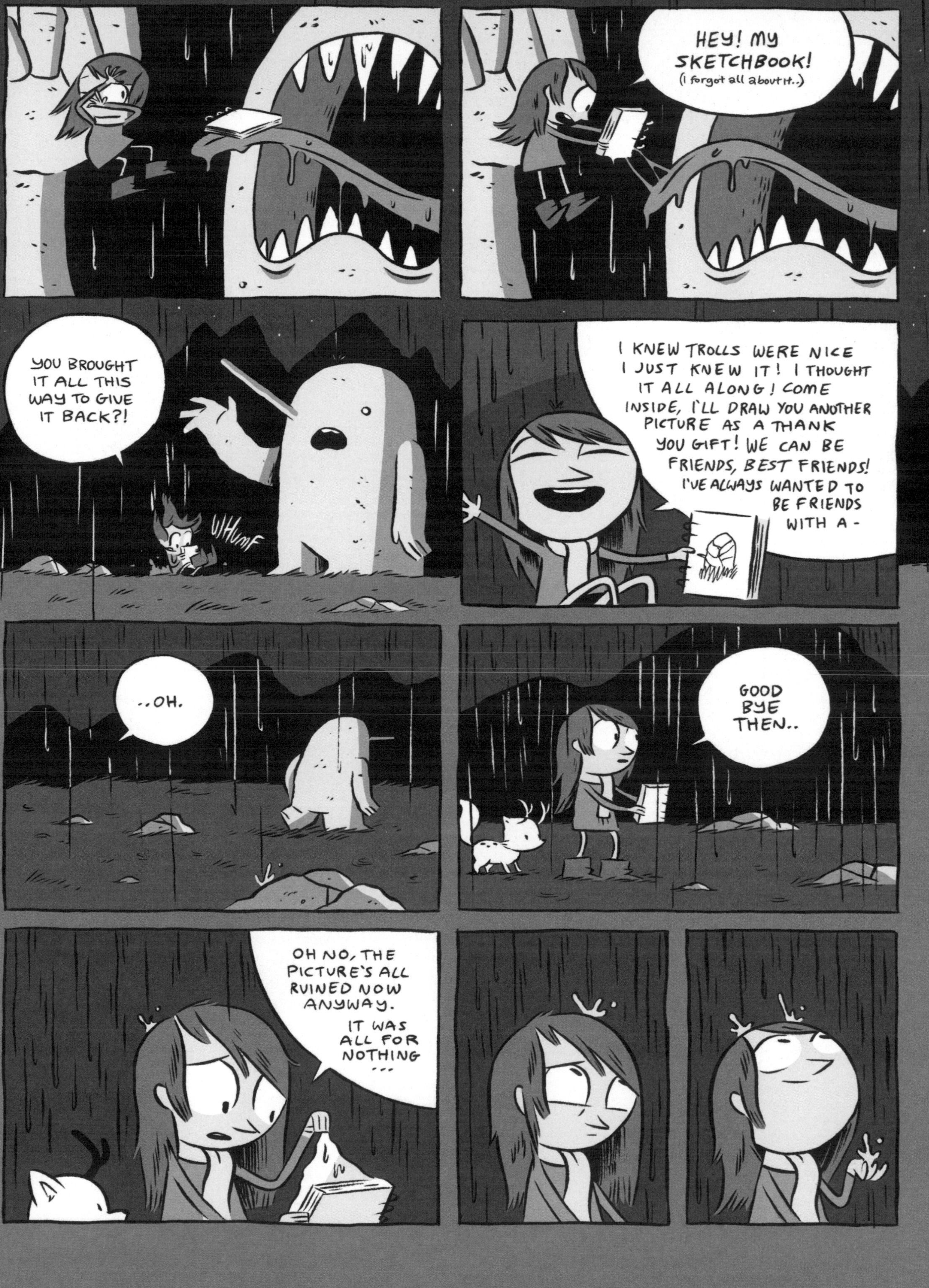
HEY! MY SKETCHBOOK!
(I forgot all about it..)
YOU BROUGHT IT ALL THIS WAY TO GIVE IT BACK?!
I KNEW TROLLS WERE NICE I JUST KNEW IT! I THOUGHT IT ALL ALONG! COME INSIDE, I'LL DRAW YOU ANOTHER PICTURE AS A THANK YOU GIFT! WE CAN BE FRIENDS, BEST FRIENDS! I'VE ALWAYS WANTED TO BE FRIENDS WITH A -
..OH.
GOOD BYE THEN..
OH NO, THE PICTURE'S ALL RUINED NOW ANYWAY.
IT WAS ALL FOR NOTHING ...

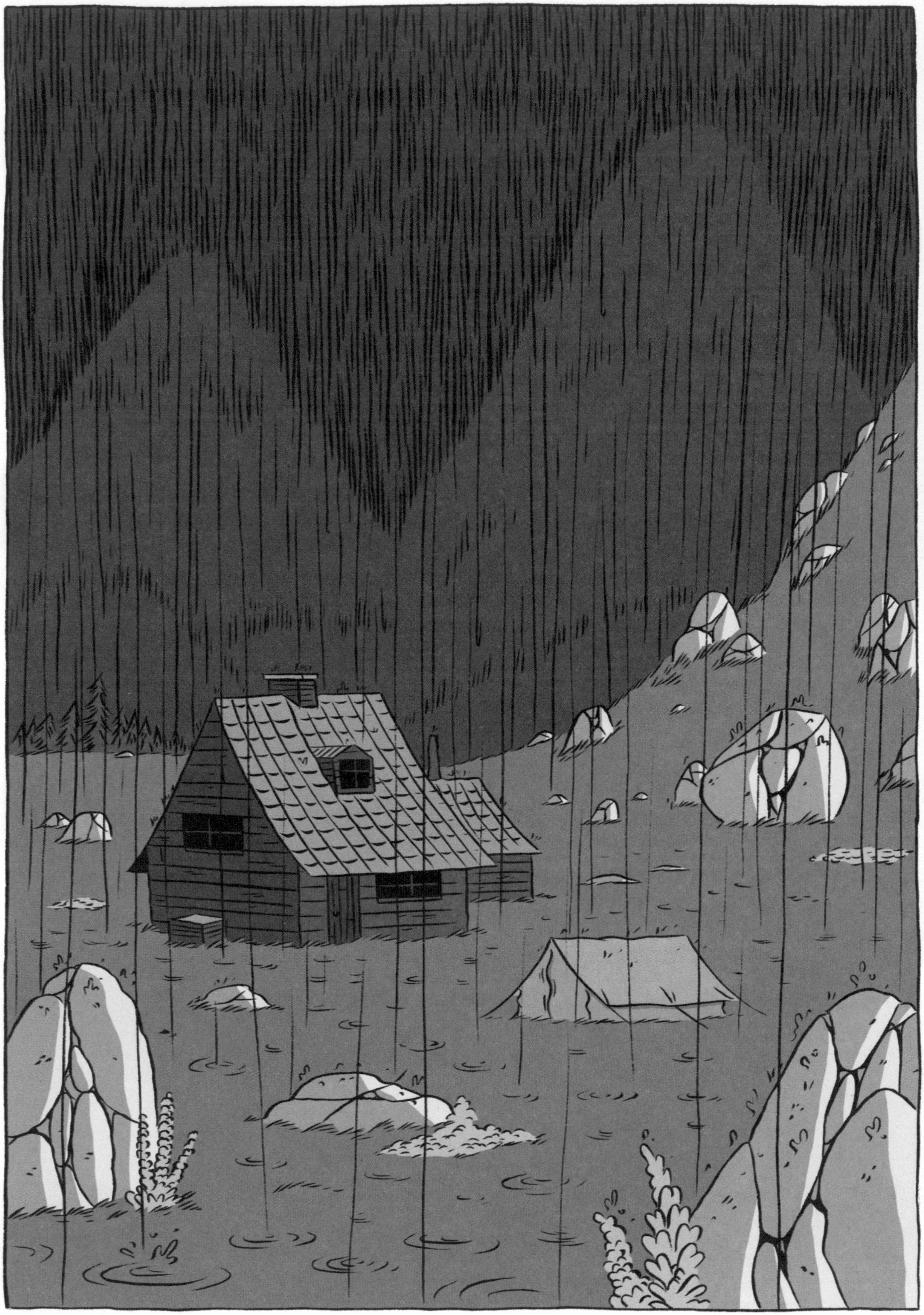

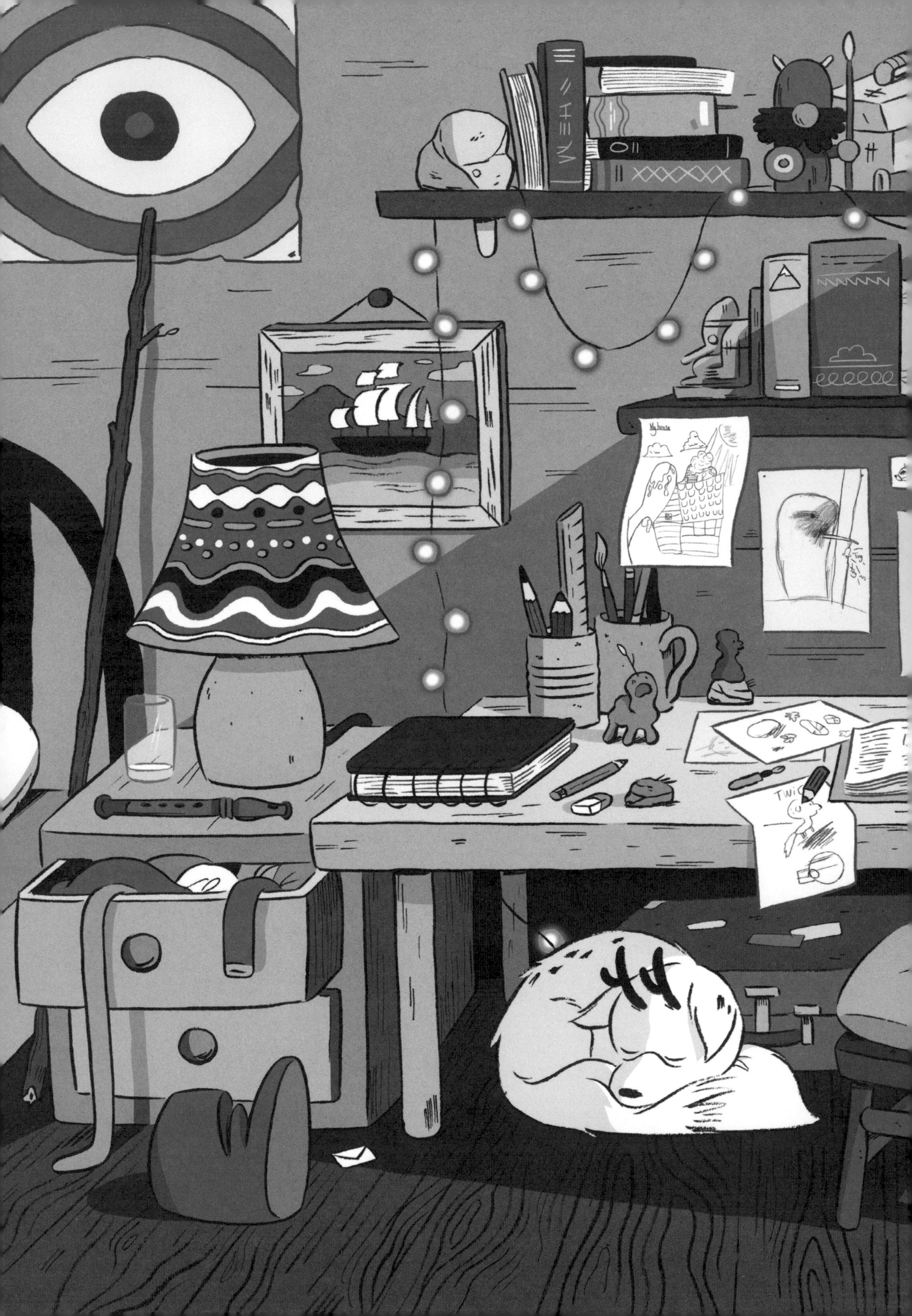
My house

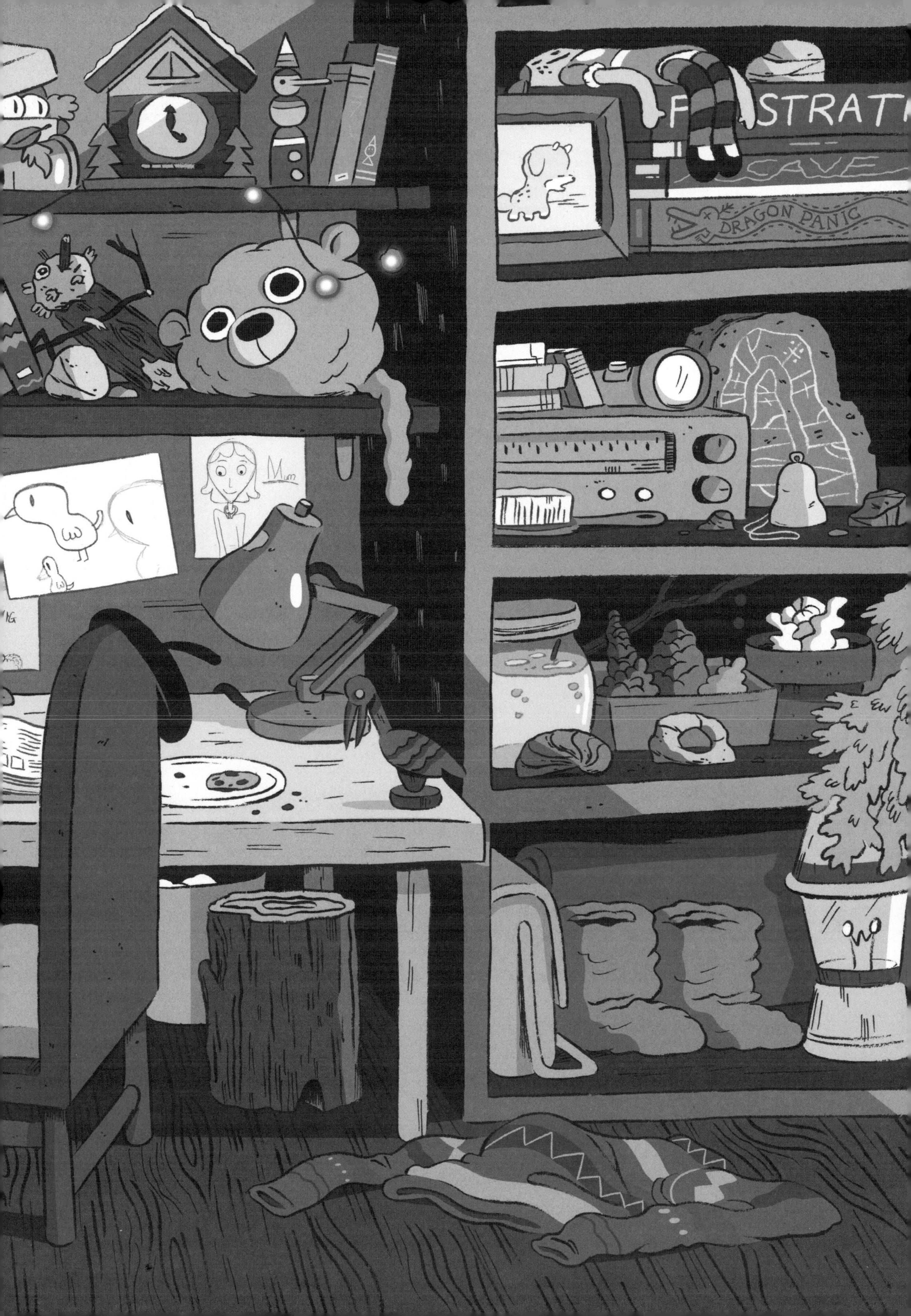

STRAT
CAVE
DRAGON PANIC
Mum

and although they will often mimic the regular stones that litter their territory, they are far from undetectable. They are frequently distinguishable by the hints of a face or the characteristically long nose, although the more devious trolls will actively attempt to conceal this feature.

Left, photograph of a petrified troll with concealed nose (photographer/date unknown). Above, an artist's interpretation of the unpetrified specimen.

The petrification process is not a pleasant or comfortable one for the rock troll, with the level of discomfort varying wildly. Larger trolls tend to take it in their stride, while for smaller and weaker specimens the effect can be permanent. It's generally accepted however that all those vulnerable to the sun's effects strive to avoid it when possible. Even those species not susceptible to petrification appear to take a dislike to it. It is for this reason that trolls tend to make their homes in the shadows of mountains, deep in forests and most commonly, in caves. Even at night it is rare to encounter a troll too far from the safety of its lair for fear of being caught out by the approaching dawn.

T ROLLS & BELLS

It has long been known that trolls have a seemingly irrational fear of the sound of ringing bells. Unlike sunlight, the sound appears to have no physiological effects on the creatures, except for those resulting directly from the psychological distress the ringing causes them.

Historically, this has been exploited to great effect by humans who have found themselves in conflict with trolls, both as a method of personal self-defence and on a larger scale. Settlers arriving in the unspoiled wildernesses around the Nornfjords would first erect temporary wooden bell towers, to secure the area in preparation for building. Cities such as Trolberg maintain a large number of permanent bell towers with a regular ringing schedule to keep the native trolls a safe distance from their walls.

In the past, travellers would hang small bells in the mouths of caves that were believed to be home to trolls, both as a warning to fellow travellers looking for shelter and to potentially prevent the trolls from leaving their lair.

Similarly, when setting up a camp, travellers would search the immediate area for suspicious looking rocks and hang a bell from any nose-like protrusions they came across. If any of the stones began to stir when night fell, the camp would be alerted. However, in recent

35

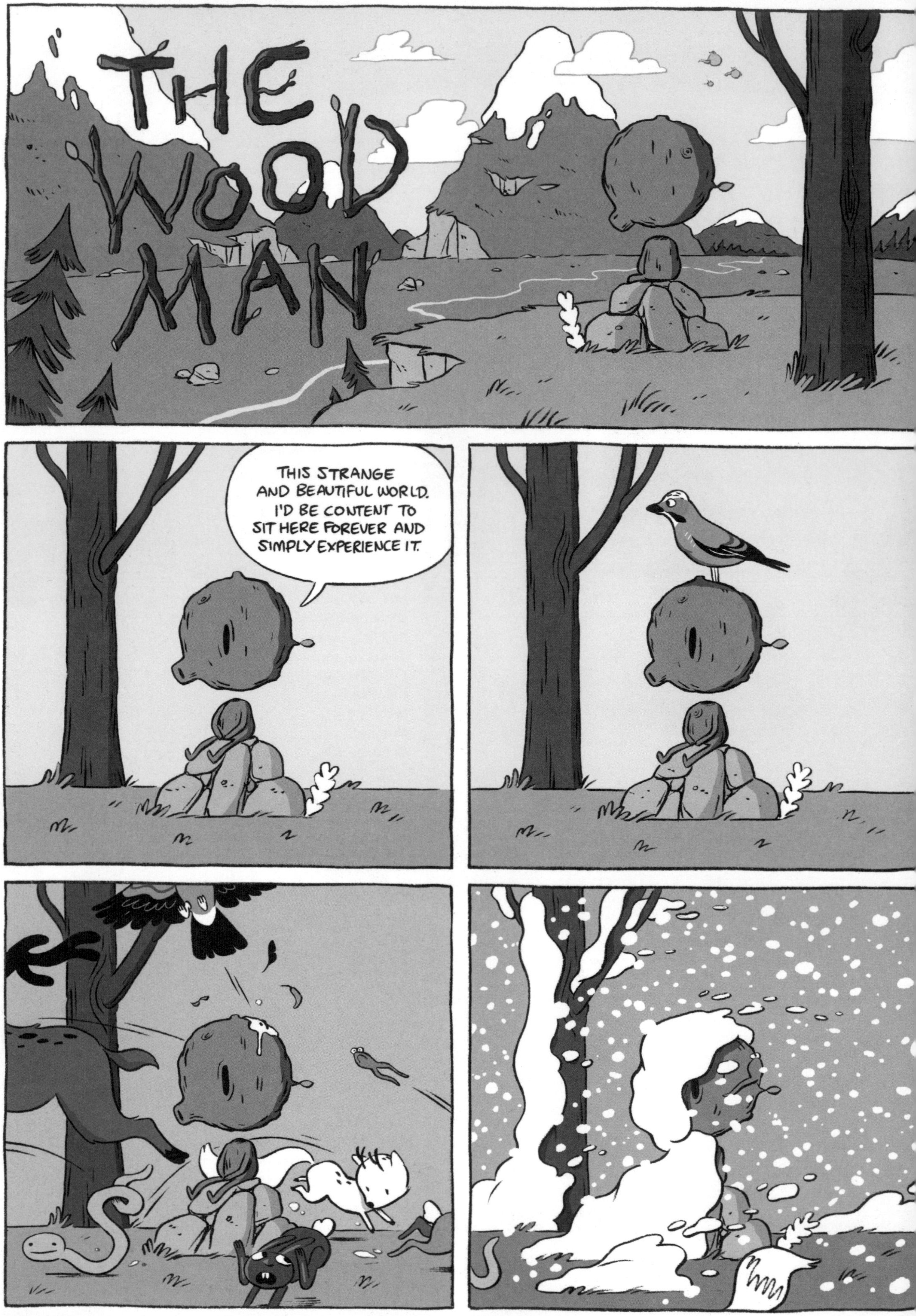
THE WOOD MAN
THIS STRANGE AND BEAUTIFUL WORLD. I'D BE CONTENT TO SIT HERE FOREVER AND SIMPLY EXPERIENCE IT.

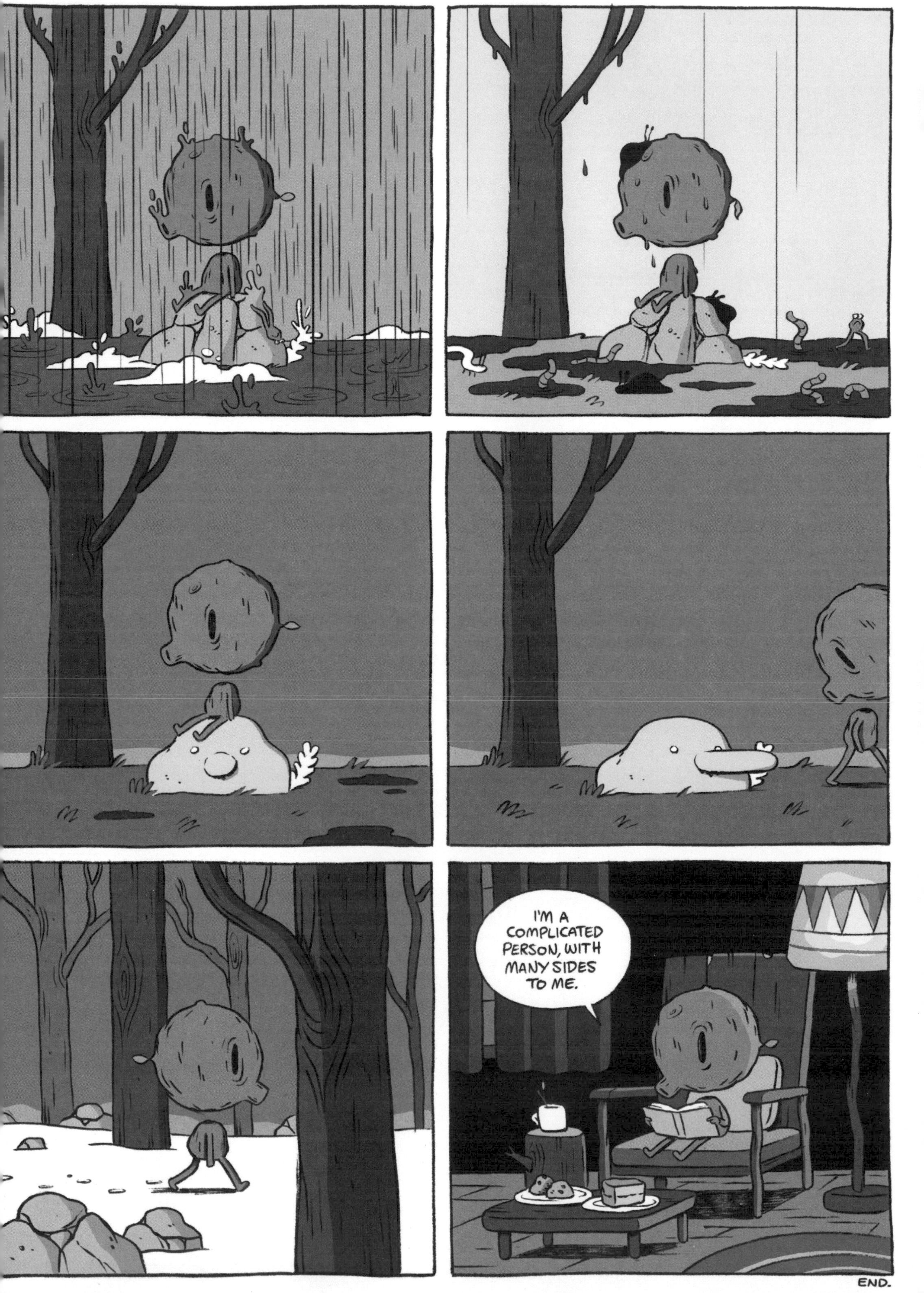
I'M A COMPLICATED PERSON, WITH MANY SIDES TO ME.
END.

SKETCHES

These are a selection of drawings from my sketchbooks, all done during the development of this comic.

-Luke

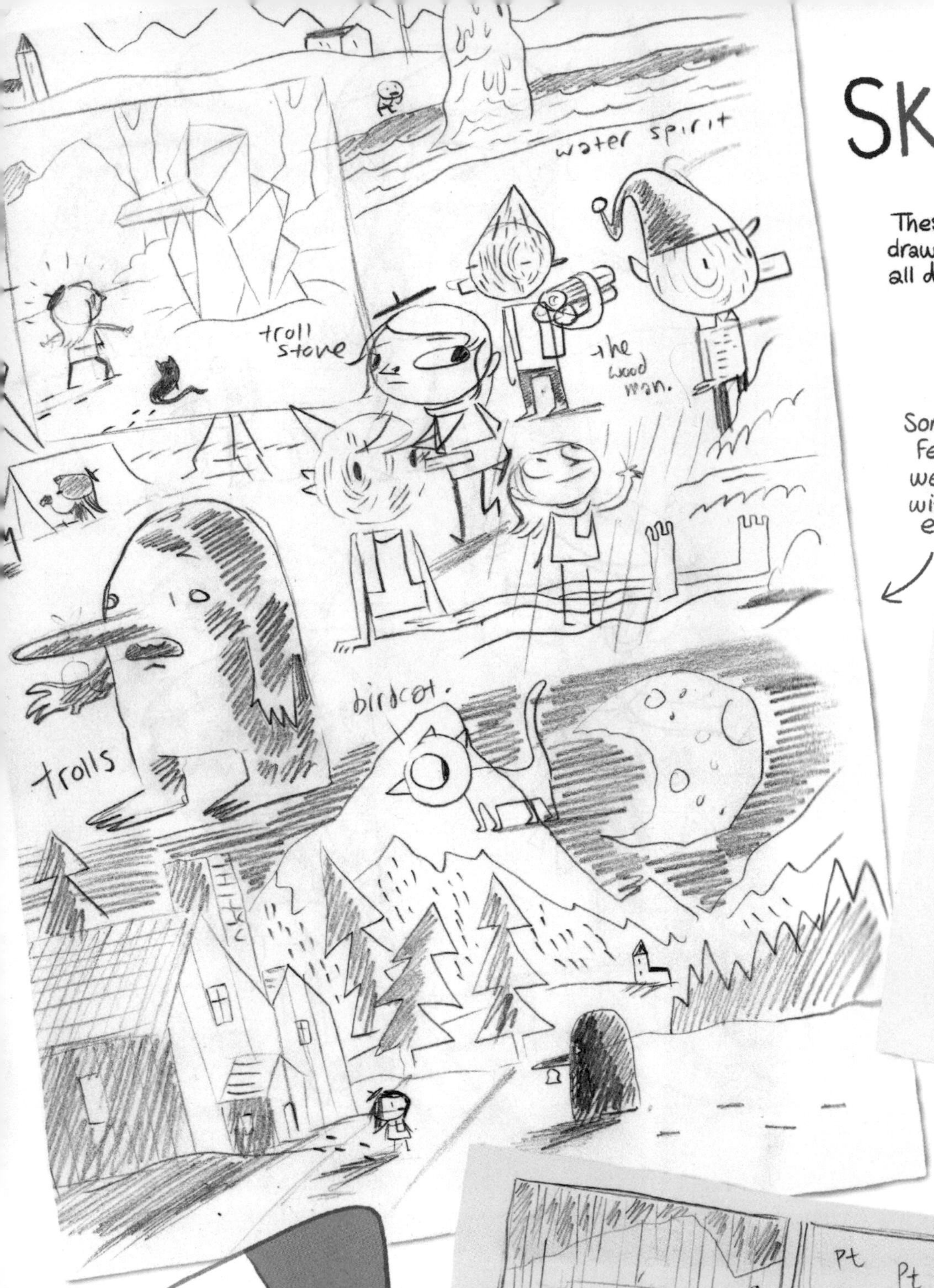

water spirit
troll stone
the wood man.
birdcat.
trolls

Some early sketches featuring the Wood Man wearing clothes and a cat with a beak who would eventually become Twig.

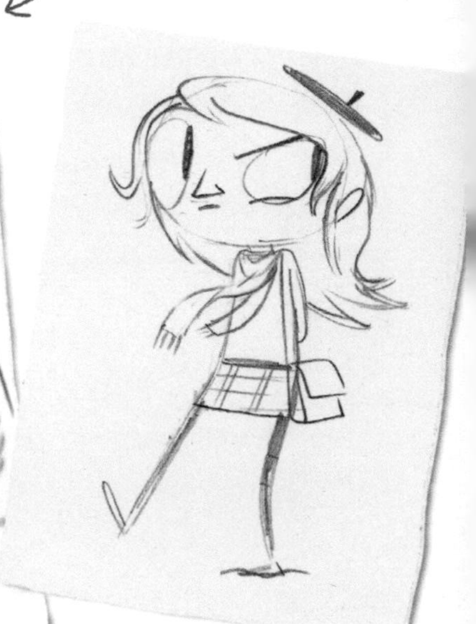

"Tall Hilda"

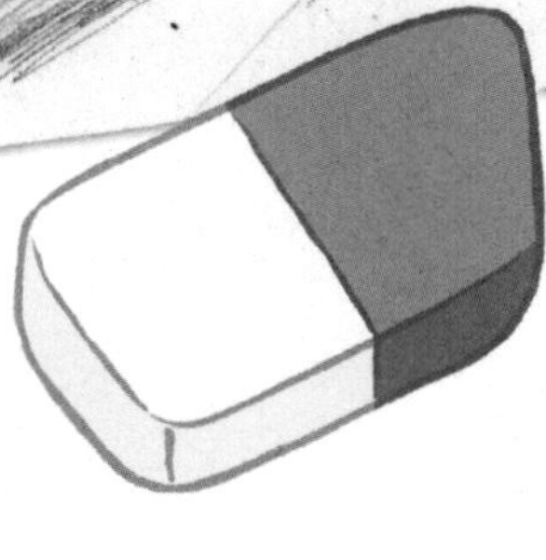

Ideas for scenes to include in the story.

This one didn't quite make it.

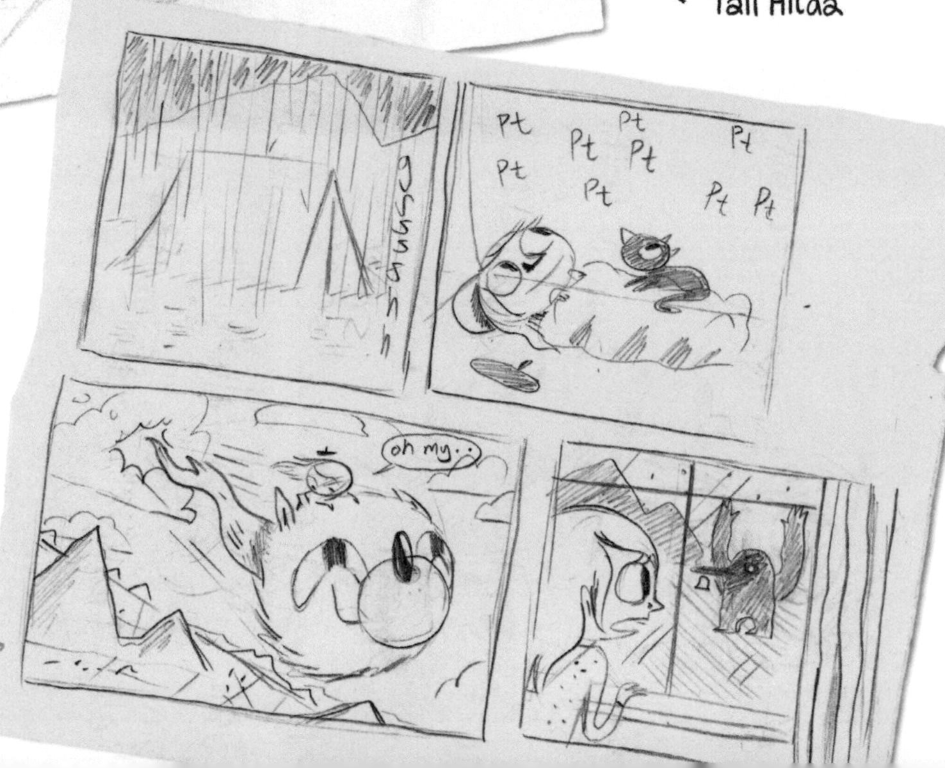

Pt Pt Pt Pt Pt Pt Pt Pt Pt
oh my..

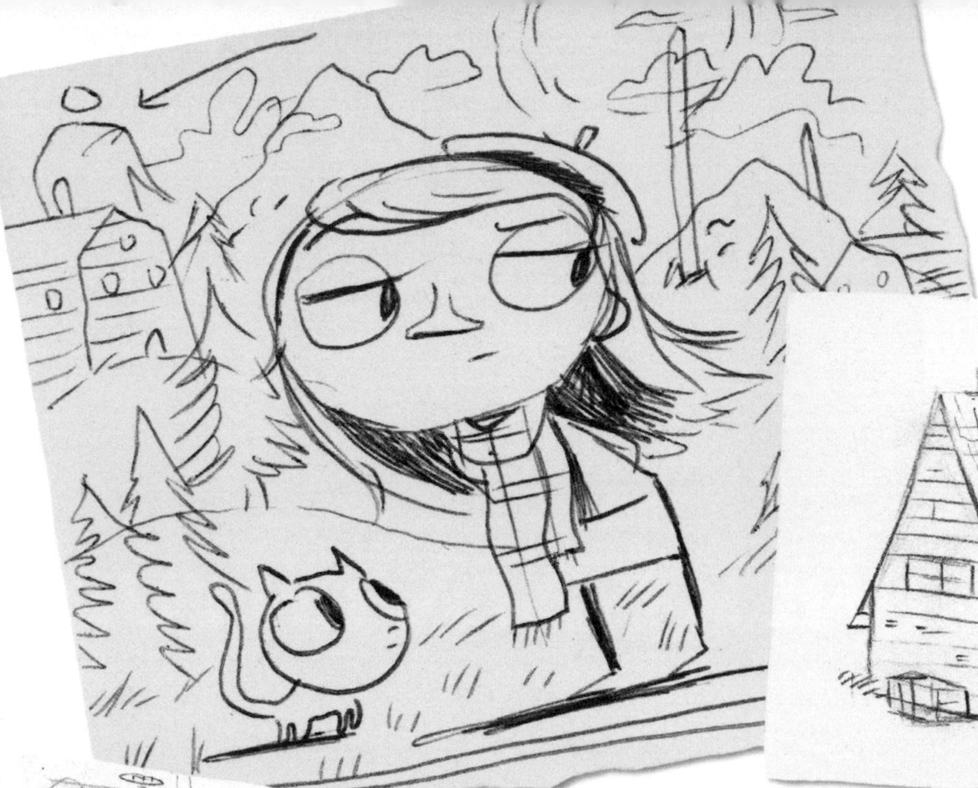

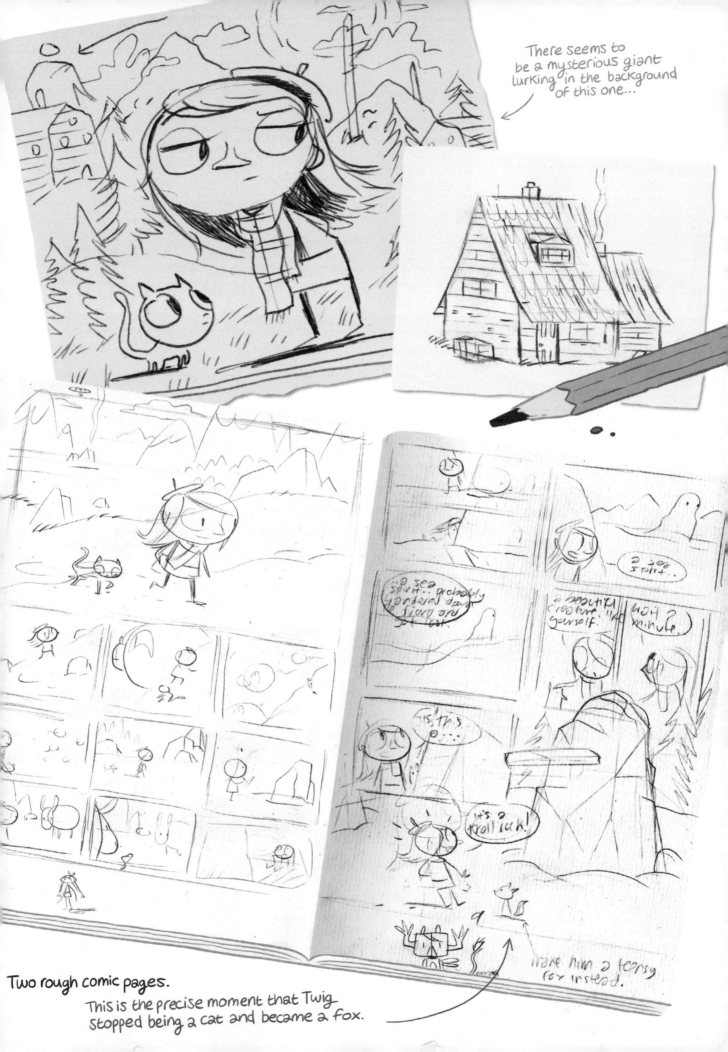

There seems to be a mysterious giant lurking in the background of this one...

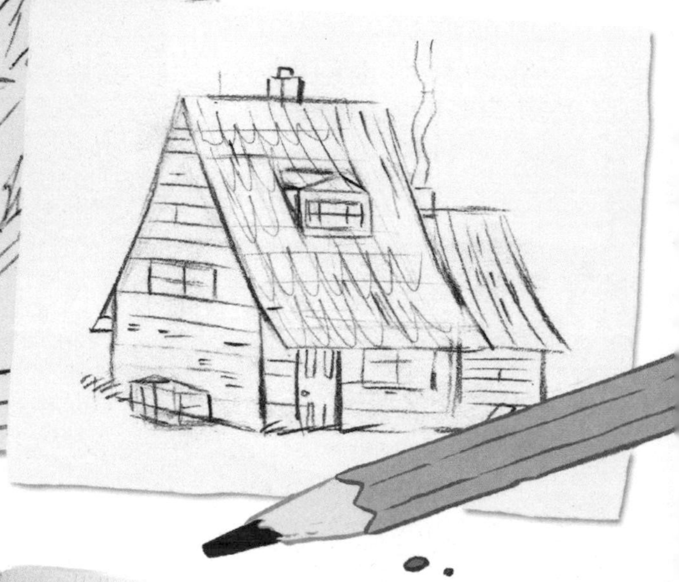

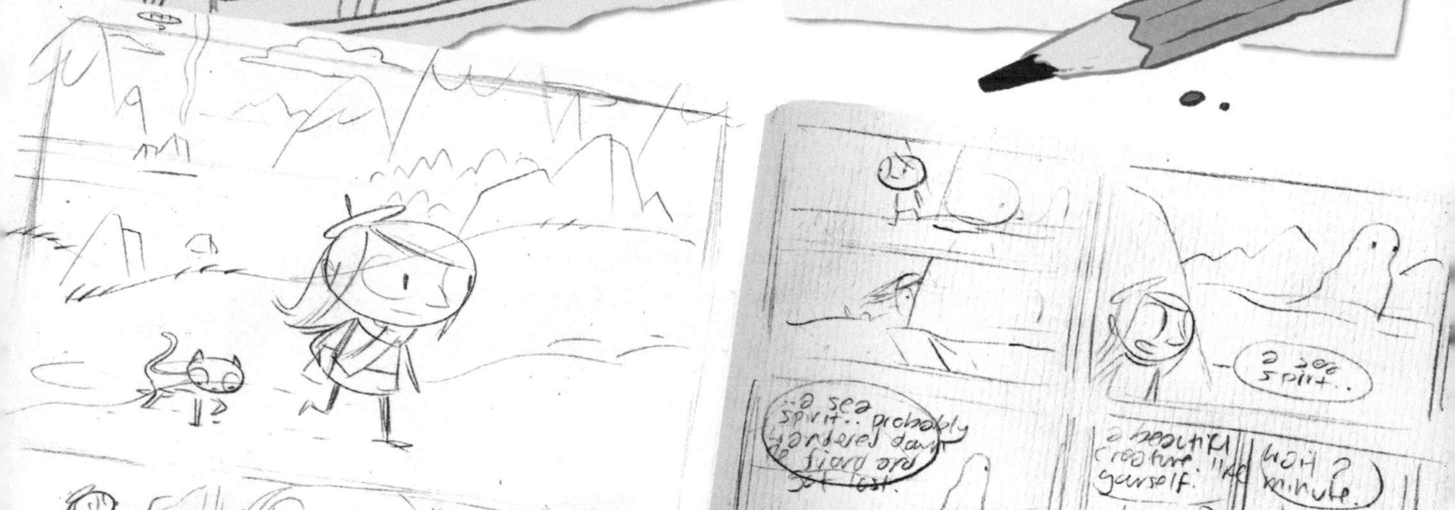
...a sea spirit.. probably wandered down the fjord and got lost.
a sea spirit..
make him a teensy fox instead.

Two rough comic pages.

This is the precise moment that Twig stopped being a cat and became a fox.

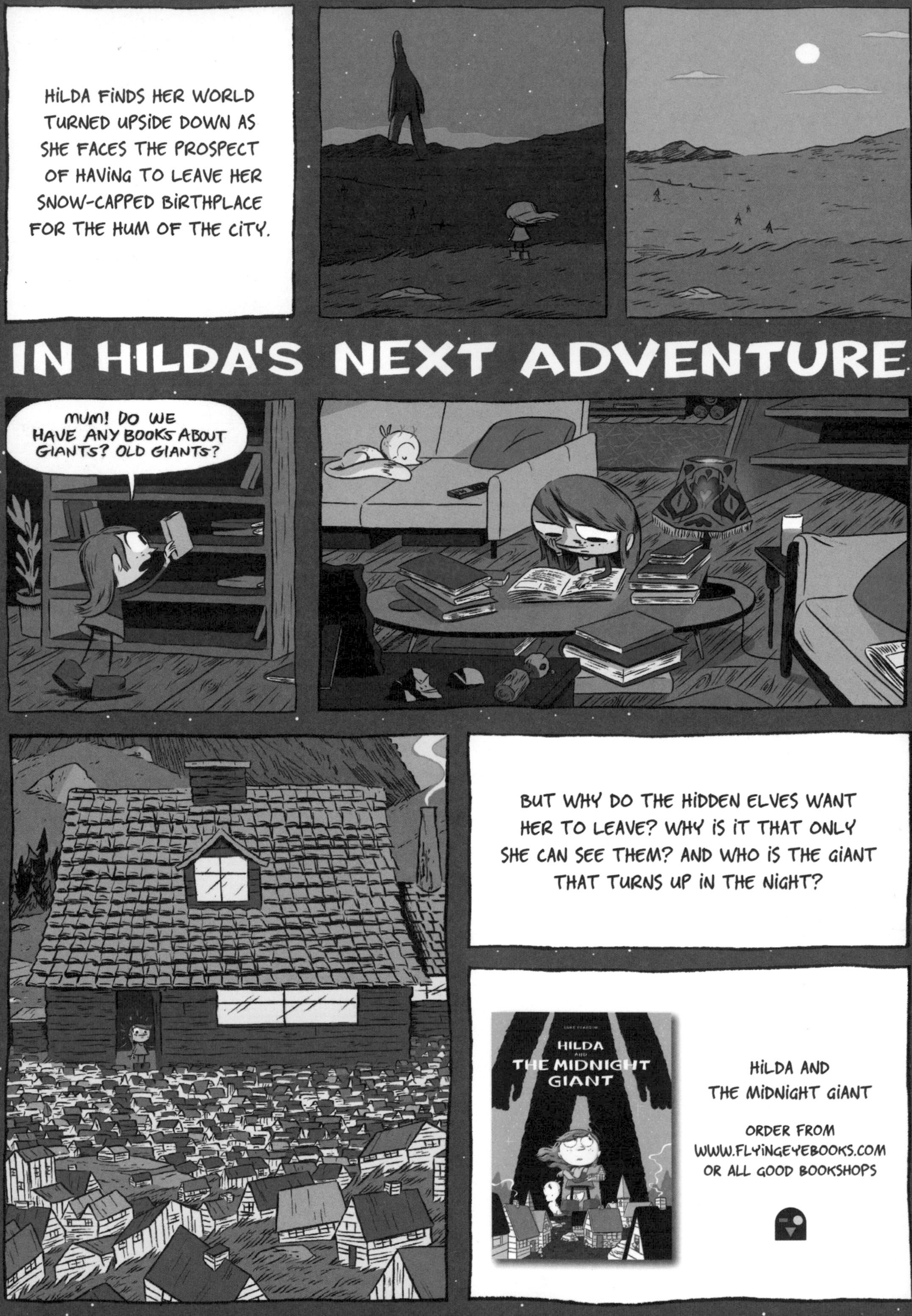

HILDA FINDS HER WORLD TURNED UPSIDE DOWN AS SHE FACES THE PROSPECT OF HAVING TO LEAVE HER SNOW-CAPPED BIRTHPLACE FOR THE HUM OF THE CITY.
IN HILDA'S NEXT ADVENTURE
MUM! DO WE HAVE ANY BOOKS ABOUT GIANTS? OLD GIANTS?
BUT WHY DO THE HIDDEN ELVES WANT HER TO LEAVE? WHY IS IT THAT ONLY SHE CAN SEE THEM? AND WHO IS THE GIANT THAT TURNS UP IN THE NIGHT?
HILDA AND THE MIDNIGHT GIANT
HILDA AND THE MIDNIGHT GIANT
ORDER FROM WWW.FLYINGEYEBOOKS.COM OR ALL GOOD BOOKSHOPS